The Perfect Match
A Reindeer Falls Holiday Romance
M. E. Bakos

For Joe and Chipper

Copyright © December 2024 by M. E. Bakos

All rights reserved.

No part of this publication may be reproduced, distributed, or transmitted in any form or by any means, including photocopying, recording, or other electronic or mechanical methods, without the prior written permission of the publisher, except as permitted by U.S. copyright law. For permission requests, contact mebakos@yahoo.com.

The story, all names, characters, and incidents portrayed in this production are fictitious. No identification with actual persons (living or deceased), places, buildings, and products is intended or should be inferred.

Chapter 1

Merry

"It's time for you to get out there and find a *real* Mr. Right," Aunt Liz announced. "I promised your mother I would look out for you after she died. I vowed you would be married to a good man by the time you turned thirty. Time's a-wasting."

We were sitting on her deck and watching the ripples on Reindeer River as we talked. Two months earlier, I had settled into the pet-friendly apartment that she had found which was about six blocks from her house. I visited often with Fido; a small terrier rescue I had adopted. In my mind, his name was short for Fidelity. I wanted a male that would be faithful and loyal. Fido was true to his name by lunging at people or larger dogs who dared come near while we strolled the river walk. I loved it.

"Aunt Liz, that is old-fashioned. Women have more freedom now; they don't have to be married."

"Do you want a family?" She crossed her arms and fixed her gaze on me.

"A child would be nice." I smiled.

"Do you want to raise a child on your own?"

"Well, no. I would want a male role model."

"Then you want a husband."

"The last one didn't work out so well," I grumbled. I was leery of getting married again. When I came by to leave my set of keys the day after moving out of the apartment Derrick and I shared, Sarah, my replacement, had answered the door. With Derrick watching in the background, I let loose a string of vile words, threw the keys over her shoulder at him, and followed with my wedding ring. It wasn't my most mature moment. But it felt good.

"He was a butthead," she said.

"Yes. He was," I admitted.

"It's time you got out," she stated. "Did the work, found a mate. You're twenty-six, fast approaching thirty. After thirty-five, you're a geriatric mother in the medical field."

"That sounds dismal." I frowned.

"It is. Let's get started. I promised your mother." She was firm and jutted her chin for emphasis. "Even if we weren't close. Family takes care of family."

"How?" I hadn't dated for five years. On a lark, my college best friend and I had set up online profiles. We were far from our small-town high schools. That was where I met Derrick. We married, and I dropped out of full-time school while he finished his degree. I supported us and planned to go back to school, after he got a good job. Then he'd taken up with the hussy, as I now called her. That was probably unfair. It takes two. He was more to blame than she was. He had made the commitment.

"I don't get it. People who go online," Aunt Liz said. "Dating sites." She sniffed. "That's how you met that last clunker," as she referred to my ex. "You could join a group."

"I hate groups. I'm an introvert."

"Yes, you are. We'll work on it." She arched one eyebrow and pursed her lips. "I'll ask my knitting club. One of my friends should have an eligible candidate."

I left her preoccupied with her mission to find me a husband and drove home with Fido. Upstairs, in my second-floor apartment in a funky 1920's brownstone, I unpacked her care package and stowed the food, then took Fido out for a stroll. The weather was turning towards a long, glorious fall, with deep red oak and yellow maple leaves. The air was crisp, and I inhaled, and admired the bounty of colors. Gazing at the scenery, we strolled back. Fido strained at his leash on the sidewalk below the steps to the building and barked furiously at a man inside the glassed entry wearing a brown jacket, and a baseball cap pulled low over his forehead.

It was Joel Connor, the maintenance man. The day I moved in, he had stuck out his hand and introduced himself, his deep dimples and kind blue eyes impressive. Charmed, I smiled at him. Since then, we had exchanged a nod and a hello as we passed each other while he worked.

This day, a sleek black cat perched on his right shoulder and rode nonchalantly. The cat stiffened and glared at Fido with luminous green eyes.

I hoisted Fido, who continued his frenzied barking and tucked him under my arm. He was portable, not quite a pocket pooch, but not too much bigger than the cat staring us down.

"Fido! Hush!" I kept my grip on him and stepped around Joel, who had opened the door for us.

"Your dog's name is Fido? Not very imaginative." Joel laughed.

"It's a nickname." I was defensive.

"This is Tom Kat," he said, nodding towards the cat. "Kat with a K; that is as far as I got with a name. He was a stray, but friendly, and adopted me." He chuckled. "I couldn't find an owner, so I made Tom Kat the next in charge of the building."

"Tom Kat," I repeated. My brows rose, and Joel's mouth stretched into a broad smile that crinkled from the corner of his twinkling eyes.

"That's it." He grinned as he held the cat while the animal burrowed into his neck. "He showed up one night. I fed him. He gulped the chow and took off. But then he knew he could get a free meal, and now he comes by every night. He sits on the fire escape outside my kitchen window and waits for his handout."

Fido had quieted and stared at the cat. Tom Kat twisted and met his gaze, unblinking, ready to do battle. My grip tight, I shifted, and said, "I was happy to find a pet-friendly building in town." The place was ideal, with its proximity to a walking path close to the riverfront and shopping a few blocks away. I could walk to my office. Fido had adapted to his new surroundings, and after eating and a stroll outside, slept on the sofa with the television tuned to cartoons. I was sure he was human, with four paws and a fur coat.

"A building that takes cats and dogs is rare." He shrugged, placing a hand on the cat.

"Yes, I suppose it is." I studied his expression and tilted my head. His tone had set off an alarm bell in my mind.

"Dogs are more vocal and need to be taken out. Sometimes they bark when they get lonely," he remarked, stroking the cat. He sniffed, and his eyes became hooded as he surveyed the dog.

"If Fido barks a lot when I'm gone, call or text me. I can usually slip out. I work about five minutes away, at the real estate management company on Main Street."

"Sure. The office has your number." He shot me a brief smile. "I have to get back to work. There's a plugged pipe in Apartment 105."

"Of course. Is that fur on your jacket?"

"Yes." He brushed the front of his coat and shrugged.

"My dog comes from a non-shedding breed of dogs." I smiled. "No fur left on clothes or anywhere in the apartment."

"Uh, huh. I have a pipe to fix," he said, and turned toward the problem unit. Tom Kat still rode his shoulder, which I noticed was nicely squared.

My apartment was wedged in the corner of the second floor of the three-story building. Built before central air conditioning, the windows were long and narrow, with radiators that hissed and gurgled with hot water that spewed heat. He often toted a toolbox for repairs in the aging building.

"Sure." I nodded and trekked the worn carpeted stairs to my place, and went inside, mulling over Joel's odd tone when he said dogs were more trouble than cats. I gave Fido a treat and said, "Please don't bark while I'm away. Joel doesn't like dogs, and we both know that black cat isn't a fan."

At least, I had gotten in a dig about cat fur. Any pet could have problems. The little dog raced away with the treat, ate it happily, then jumped on the couch and burrowed into the throw for a nap.

Joel

She is cute, I will give her that. I glanced back at the new tenant as she flounced up the stairs to her apartment with that yappy little dog and smirked. Her big brown eyes hung on to every word I'd said about the problems with having dogs in an apartment. She flipped her long hair back and jutted her jaw as she pushed back about her mutt.

Why the Goldmans agreed to rent to a tenant with a dog baffled me. They said it was going to be a trial to see if dogs would benefit the bottom line. A happy tenant was a long-term tenant. My hands were tied. Fido was not much bigger than Tom Kat but a lot more work. What was the big deal about a little fur? Ha! She delivered the snark with a bit of honey, but I saw the chip on her shoulder. Her back stiffened when I lectured her about dogs. Mark my word, that mutt was going to be a problem. Along with his mistress, Merry Ernst.

I would not have it, *couldn't* have it. The Goldmans' buildings were going to be the best in town. If residents had to listen to a dog barking, it would bust my chances at making this deal. Tenants would leave, and the Goldmans could renege on our agreement to purchase the buildings.

Great looking wasn't everything. I learned that from Patricia, my former fiancée. She was a fox with silky blonde hair who came on like gangbusters when I had the corporate gig. We rode a roller coaster ride of highs and lows. The lowest of lows came when I left the corporate world, and she turned from white hot to 'I need more time' and gave back my engagement ring. She had hinted the diamond solitaire was small, swept her marvelous long hair aside, and with a wry smile murmured, "Cute." Then she threw her arms around me, kissed me passionately, and whispered, "We'll go shopping. You'll be an executive soon."

When I left my job for a chance to own my business, she needed 'space.' That hurt. The rejection and pain nearly brought me to my knees. The weeks following were a blur. No more women for me. Even cute feisty ones.

Chapter 2

Merry

It was after dinner the following Wednesday that Aunt Liz phoned. I was about to take Fido out.

"Are you busy?" Her voice was filled with excitement and hinted of mystery.

"Maybe." I was wary. "What's up?"

"I have someone I want you to meet."

I groaned; my shoulders tensed.

"You don't waste any time," I countered. Glad she couldn't see my eye roll.

"Don't be such a stick in the mud. He could be the perfect husband for you," she trilled. "He's the son of one of my club women." She belonged to a monthly knitting club with a few women in her neighborhood. They called themselves the Nifty Knitters. She seldom volunteered what projects they were creating, and I doubted they did many. It was more of a social club under the pretext of yarn. "He is handsome, in a swarthy way. An engineer, with a great job and a brilliant future. He's your age." She huffed, and said pointedly, "Approaching thirty."

"There isn't anything that says thirty is over the hill for a relationship," I protested. "Besides, I'm only twenty-six."

"Your fertility is diminishing." She sniffed, and added, "As we speak."

"Aunt Liz!"

"Well, it's true. You don't want to end up like me without an heir to handle your affairs later in life." Her husband, Alvin, had passed, and they never had children. She had always treated me like a daughter.

"I will take care of your affairs, Auntie. Promise."

"I know you will, but I still want you to find a good husband and have a family."

"What about you? You're still young enough to remarry. Fifty is the new forty," I countered.

"No, Merry. Another mate is *not* in the cards," she said. "It's your time."

In a burst of courage as a teenager, sensing it was an off-limit topic, I had asked her about their lack of offspring. She shut me down with a look and a raised eyebrow, saying, "Alvin and I couldn't have children." It was only now, when she became focused on finding a new spouse for me, the geriatric age of motherhood came up.

I loved Aunt Liz. I knew her heart was in the right place, and I could stand to get out.

"What do you mean by 'swarthy'?"

"Sophia is of proud Italian heritage." I heard a deep sigh from the other end of the phone. "She is a devoted mother and showed the group his college graduation photo. The man is on the short, stocky, Italian side. Think Sylvester Stallone in his younger days."

"That doesn't sound terrible. I'm not quite five-foot-four," I reasoned. Well, maybe five-feet-two and a half.

"I haven't met him. Mind you, Sophia has a forceful personality," she mused.

I flinched as I considered myself with an extrovert.

"Do opposites really attract?" I asked. She ignored my question, and Fido raised his head long enough to gaze at me steadily, then snuggled back into the sofa.

"She's bringing him to my house for the club tonight. I want you to come."

"Oh! I'm sorry I forgot. I have a thing. Maybe another time. Fido is begging to go out," I said in a rush. "I need to go."

"What thing?" she asked as I clicked off.

"That was close," I muttered, and went to lower the living room window. Earlier, I had raised it for sunlight and a late summer breeze. Closing the window, I looked down at the parking lot. Joel was loading tree branches from a recent storm into the bed of his white pickup. He dragged a branch across the lot from the sidewalk to his truck. Tom Kat pranced behind, tail high, and pounced on the tree limb as Joel strode. Joel glanced up at my window. Our gazes locked. Startled, I gasped. A spark lit my senses, and I quickly drew the shade. Flustered, I ducked out the front entry with Fido, avoiding him and his cat.

***

The next day at work, I made out the day's deposit for the rent checks. Many tenants paid by direct deposit, but there were a few holdouts with paper checks. I entered the checks and tallied the deposit. The phone rang, interrupting my computations.

"How about an early dinner?" It was Aunt Liz. "Maybe grab a bite at that new Asian place." Her tone was casual, and I was relieved she didn't mention the knitting club.

"Sure." I checked the hour. "About five-thirty? I get off at four-thirty and after a quick walk home to feed Fido and take him out, that would be perfect."

"You're a good dog mom," she observed.

"Thanks." I laughed. "He keeps me on my toes."

"He's a good boy. I'll meet you there." She hung up. I finished out the day, dropped the deposit into the safe, and left for home. Midway up the staircase to the second floor, I heard barking. Racing the rest of the way, I unlocked the door and burst inside.

"Fido!"

His paws were on the windowsill in the kitchen, and his body shook with the intensity of his barks. From the entry,

I saw a black cat on the fire escape outside the kitchen window. Tom Kat sat on his haunches unperturbed and licked a front paw, casting a glare at Fido as he yelped. I had left the shade up, as the view was the brick side of the building next to mine. Hurriedly, I lowered the shade to block Fido's view of the peeping cat. Scooping the dog up, I stroked him. "It's okay, it's only the cat. He can't reach you."

A hard rap came at the door. Checking the security peephole, it was Joel, and he did not look happy.

Oh, great. I opened the door with Fido in my grip.

"Your dog was barking and creating a disturbance." His nose twitched and his mouth puckered, as if he was holding back a torrent of accusations. "Another resident complained."

"He was barking at your cat!" My arms circled Fido protectively. "Tom Kat was sitting outside my kitchen window peeping, provoking him!" I sputtered. "Who complained?"

Joel's eyes flashed with laughter, and he snorted. "I can't tell you who reported the dog." With a smirk, he said, "Tom Kat window peeping; I thought my place was the only window he peeped." After another chuckle, he said, "I'll watch for him. If I hear barking, I'll check your fire escape. But if it's not Tom Kat and Fido doesn't stop, I have to give you a written warning. Three warnings, and you and the dog will be evicted. It is the owners' policy."

"I understand." My face flushed a bright red, and I shut the door, ignoring the twinge in my stomach when his gaze flicked between me and Fido. The man was a cad, and I felt sheepish, hating that I felt an attraction.

"Let's get your chow." I busied myself preparing his food, still upset. After feeding him and getting water, I stroked Fido's head.

"Keeping the shade down will help. What you can't see, can't bug you. Right?" He licked his chops, appreciative of his food, and my caution about the cat lounging outside window.

My mind raced, wondering who would have complained, and I settled on the musician who lived above me on the third floor. He worked late hours and must have heard the commotion. That would be Apartment 305. The resident handyman lived next to him in Number 307. Maybe he had gone next door to Joel and complained.

I had met the musician briefly in the entry while we were each getting our mail. He appeared to be a genial, dark-haired Hispanic man who had introduced himself and welcomed me to the building. Offering a card with the name of his band, he invited me to his next gig. He didn't seem to be a complainer, but if he slept during the day and worked nights, he might be.

Fido finished his food, and after checking the time, I leashed him, grabbed a baggie, and headed out for a potty break. I was late for meeting Aunt Liz, but it couldn't be helped.

Chapter 3

Merry

I BREEZED INTO THE restaurant fifteen minutes late and told the greeter that I was meeting someone. She pointed towards a booth where Aunt Liz waved me over, and a young man with his back to me turned and smiled a greeting. He was handsome in a roguish way. Solidly built, with a full dark beard. I hesitated, my gut churning. *She did not invite Sophia's son!*

"Merry, this is Nico. He's the young man I told you about."

Oh, yes. She did. I composed myself.

"Nice to meet you." I gave my aunt as much of a glare as I dared, took a deep breath, and scooted in next to her. "Nico is a nickname?"

"Yes. It is short for Nicolas. I am Italian. Good to meet you." He nodded; his brown eyes were firm. "We are a big family."

"I'm sorry to be late. There was a kerfuffle with Fido."

"What happened?" Aunt Liz asked.

"Fido?" The young man sipped a coke and studied me. My hair was likely a frizz of curls. I hadn't checked the mirror before dashing out of the house and had jogged the two blocks to the restaurant.

"Fido is my dog. He was barking while I was at work. The building manager said someone complained." I scanned the menu and let out a sigh.

"You have a dog? In an apartment?" Nico asked. His mouth tight.

I looked at Aunt Liz, frowning. "Yes, I have a dog. We live in an apartment."

"He isn't in the habit of barking?" she asked with a small frown.

"No, he is not. He sleeps most of the day. At least, I think he does. And it wasn't his fault! It was all Tom Kat's doing!"

"Tom Kat?" The bearded young man leaned back, coughed, and checked his cellphone.

"Tom Kat?" Aunt Liz echoed.

"He's a stray the building maintenance man adopted. Or the cat adopted him. Anyway, he has an annoying habit of lounging on the fire escape and peering into apartments. He picked mine today, and Fido saw him. It freaked him out, and he barked."

"Well, a dog is going to bark. That is what a dog does. The building owners know that when they accept dogs," she reasoned.

Nico coughed lightly and viewed his phone again, and said, "I must leave." He looked up from his phone. "I am sorry about your problem with the dog. I am allergic to most animal fur, cats, dogs, feathers." He shrugged.

"Oh? Your mother never mentioned that." Aunt Liz's voice was high and wavered with disappointment.

"Yes. Well, it is a topic that doesn't get much discussion while knitting." He grinned. "At least, I hope not. It has been wonderful meeting you, Merry. I trust everything will work out with your, uh, kerfuffle." He held out his hand for a shake. I stood, grasped his hand, and saw that I had two inches on him. Not a deal breaker. I am short, but he was shorter. Never judge a book by its cover. Allergies were the real deal breakers. Love me, love my dog, was my motto.

"It was nice meeting you," I said.

"So sorry that you have to go," Aunt Liz said, and remembering her manners, gave Nico a big smile.

After he left, I slid onto the bench across from her. "He is allergic?"

"Hmm. I guess." Her turquoise eyes narrowed, and she looked over her reading glasses. She had recently started wearing an assortment of over-the-counter readers. There was purple, pink, brown, and today's color, black plastic. She wore her shoulder-length brown locks highlighted, and she had the same wave in her hair, tending to curly, as mine did. As it was, we resembled one another. "She has never mentioned allergies in all the time we've been meeting."

"It's like he said, 'It's not a topic of conversation.'"

"Hmm. Sophia will hear from me." She wrinkled her nose and rubbed it with a curved finger, displaying a manicured nail.

"Don't. Please." I cringed at the possibility that my lack of spouse or significant other was a topic of her club get-togethers. "If it is meant to be, it will be," I quipped, trying to dispel the determined look on her face.

"Yes." She came back to the present and set her menu aside. "Nico isn't the only fish in the sea."

"Now you're scaring me." My brows rose, and I shuddered.

She sent me a little cat-ate-the-canary smile and slipped off her reading glasses.

"Let's order. I will have the Chow Mein. How about you?"

I scanned the menu, then shut it. "Egg foo young. How about some wontons?"

"They *are* yummy," she said. We gave our orders to the server and took in the fresh décor of the restaurant with gleaming lacquer tables and comfortable black padded, high back booths. Pink ornamental flowers in a glass vase decorated the front counter.

"Nice place," I said.

"Yes, they should do well." Sitting back, she surveyed the restaurant and said, "So, Nico is not the one. It just means we are one step closer to finding you the perfect match." Her eyes sparkled with determination.

"You can't be serious about finding a husband for me," I protested.

"Oh, look! Here's our food," she said. "Have a wonton." She smiled, and I could almost see the gears in her mind turning.

***

After meeting with Aunt Liz, I went home. Joel stood in the entry, his back against the wall next to the line of mailboxes in the small entry, as if he were waiting for someone.

"Hello?" I asked tentatively. Fido *couldn't* be barking again. He had looked so comfortable when I left.

"There is a spot between the buildings for residents to take their pets for elimination," he said. His gaze was serious as he studied my appearance. He squelched the start of a grin and cleared his throat.

"Yes?" I was dutiful about where I took Fido and didn't know where this conversation was headed. "That's where we go."

"And there's a garbage can for pet waste." His mouth twitched; lips pressed.

"Yes." I frowned.

"It isn't the recycling bin." He met my stare.

"Oh!" Embarrassed that I had goofed in my haste to meet up with my aunt. "I'm sorry. It won't happen again."

He offered a slow smile that started at his mouth, displayed deep dimples, and traveled to his eyes. "I'll let it go today. Fido has been in enough trouble for one day."

"Appreciate it." I gritted my teeth, as he slipped out the door to the street. *Sheesh*. Two encounters in one day with Joel had set my nerves on edge. Maybe it was best to look for another place to live. The trouble was, my budget was saying a firm 'no,' and I had already enrolled in a night class once a week.

With my class schedule set and the apartment within walking distance to my office, it was affordable. Any farther away, my aging Ford sedan would need to be replaced, not to mention the wear and tear on my body. I'd have to be more careful and dodge Joel, the dog-despiser, as I grimly coined him.

Joel

I knew that mutt would be a problem. Besides yapping and lunging, trying to take a chunk out of me, his poop was a health hazard to other residents. Three warnings and it won't be long before the Goldmans will give the dog the boot. It's too bad; Merry will go with him. Seeing how defensive she gets and the way she coddles that dog tells me she'll split in a heartbeat. And I'll have an open rental on my hands.

Fido? What kind of name is that? If she wasn't so danged hot, I would say good riddance, but that woman is sexy. Her soft smile and rosy complexion tugs at emotions I thought were long gone. But she has a 'hands off' attitude, and I had better watch my step. I do not need any complications being the building super. I have to prove myself to the Goldmans and close the deal on the buildings. No woman is going to stop me from owning the properties. Certainly not this woman. Or *that* dog.

Chapter 4

Merry

THURSDAY MORNING, A WEEK later, the time flew while I worked. Between entering data, I sneaked glances at the people who went into meetings in the office behind me. There were rumblings of a takeover, but I wasn't part of the water cooler gossip. Kristina Joy Young, the office manager, and a friend, had clued me in to a possible buyout.

"Big news, Merry." She rolled over in her chair from the next desk and stopped, breathless. Her tone was hushed, and her ample body trembled with excitement. Pushing red curls behind her ears and stabbing tortoise shell-colored frames up the bridge of her nose, she peered at me and said, "The big wigs have new accounts for us to handle. A couple of buildings near the riverfront, close to where you live." She frowned. "Mr. Bigg dropped off these records this morning. He wants the accounts set up in the computer." She laid a fat manilla envelope on my desk.

"No problem. Am I ever going to meet Mr. Bigg?" The running joke in the office was that Mr. Bigg, like his name, was too important to meet with the staff. He worked only with Benjamin, the company's portfolio manager, who was a gangly six-foot-five, dark-haired man with a sly smile. Mr. Bigg mysteriously called ahead and left his documents with him before the rest of the staff arrived.

"Word is that if any of us met him, Benjamin would have to kill us." Her expression was deadpan, and I blinked. "Just kidding." She let out a belly laugh. "You should have seen the look on your face."

"Not funny," I muttered.

"You need to have more fun." She laughed.

Kris and I had become fast friends. She had held my hand when I told her about Derrick and our breakup. She had covered for me when I had to meet with my lawyer and consoled me with the failure of my happily ever-after. Not one to waste time on a failed relationship, she was pragmatic; she confided she had been married and divorced three times by age thirty. Now, she was happily single at thirty-five and on board with Aunt Liz's advice. "Forget the jerk and move on. There's a better man coming," she had said, and added, "I'd love to be a nanny." I looked at her, puzzled. "Not full time, of course. But it takes a village."

"Great, now I have two matchmakers," I had muttered. "Nothing like pressure."

"How was dinner with your aunt? Has she found your Mr. Right yet?"

I groaned. "You would ask."

"Well?" she prompted.

"She invited the son of one of her knitting clubbers to dinner with us."

"Nice. Quick work." She chuckled. I glared, and she backed off.

"He's allergic to animal fur and feathers. Or says he is. He might have been looking for an escape." I shrugged.

"Yeah, men can be cagey." She nodded vigorously. "Allergies would be a deal breaker with a dog or for any future pets." She asked, "Do you think it was an easy out for him?"

"Or he wasn't keen on a taller woman in his life," I mused.

Her eyes narrowed, and she asked, "He was shorter than you?"

"Yep."

"Well, if that's his attitude, then to heck with him." She added, "Besides, it's a proven statistic that tall men make more money than short men."

"How does that work with women?" I asked.

"Same deal. Oh, and it helps if you're blonde." She looked pointedly at my hair. "You could highlight it, like your aunt does." Aunt Liz was a frequent visitor at my office and had met Kris.

"So, if I go blonde and grow a few inches, I'd make more money and meet the man of my dreams," I teased.

"Couldn't hurt." She grinned, her eyes flashing emerald green.

"I think I will stay single and happy with Fido. Short is fine, and works for me," I said loftily and fluffed my hair. We both laughed.

"Single is not so bad," Kristina agreed. About then Benjamin, who I thought could be a double for the actor, Jeff Goldblum, strolled from his office and paused, towering above us. He eased on to the edge of my desk, crossed his arms, and observed us with a crafty smile.

"Kristina gave you the new accounts to set up?" He shifted his gaze between us. He was massive, and his bum took up one side of my desk. I rolled my chair back.

Benjamin wore thick black eyeglasses. His dark hair was short and gelled with spikes, and he spoke in a low tone. "Bigg is an important client. I want everyone to impress him with our work ethic and have his accounts in order when you leave today."

"I'm on it," I said.

Kris rose and slid her chair to her desk. Her face flushed, embarrassed by Benjamin's directive.

"Got it, boss." she saluted. I sensed a spark between the two, but in front of me, they appeared all business.

By the end of the day, I had entered the new accounts into the computer, ordered checks, and emailed Benjamin, saying all was done. Kris was correct that the new buildings, each with their own ledgers and building names, were in my neighborhood. Mr. Bigg was gaining more and more real estate, primarily apartment buildings. My building was owned by an elderly couple, Mr. and Mrs. Goldman, who might want to sell their properties. If I hazarded a guess as to their ages, I would put them over the age of 65, but I couldn't be sure.

I hustled to wrap up the day's work and clean my desk.

"Do you have class tonight?" Kris slipped on her jacket and grabbed her handbag.

"Yes." Running late as usual. Thursday night's class was a break from the business classes I had taken when Derrick and I were together. A design class, taken at the local community college, gave my mind a needed break from the routine of my job. There was just enough time to get home, walk Fido, drive to the school, park, and get to my class. I would take a sandwich to tide me over on the drive. Fido would not be happy that I would be away again, but it was a short day tomorrow and I could make it up to him then.

"See you." I waved to Kris, and speed-walked home.

"Yay, Friday!" She waved goodbye and tossed her head, curls bouncing.

Fido was waiting at the door as I brushed in. I leashed him as he excitedly licked my face, and we ran down the stairs and out the back exit to the pet area. We returned, taking the same route. I snatched him up, spotting Joel with the black cat riding his shoulder in the lobby. Fido's ears perked up, and he let out a small bark as the pair left.

"That was close," I whispered and cuddled the small dog. He whimpered and looked at me with big brown eyes. Once home, I undid his leash and put his chow down. I changed into jeans, a plaid flannel shirt, and a hoodie, and grabbed my backpack, already loaded with that night's notebook. It would be a lecture by a local artist, and I was looking forward to hearing about his life. I wanted to pursue art as a career. Balancing accounts was a job. I wanted something more.

Fido hopped on the sofa and resigned, laid down, sensing I was about to leave.

"Tomorrow afternoon is all yours," I promised him. Petting him, I felt guilty about leaving again. Thursdays were the longest day he had without a human. I had thought of asking Aunt Liz or Kris to stay with him and made a mental note to follow up on that possibility. Ducking Joel and worrying about Fido's behavior when I was gone was taking a toll.

Joel

I played dumb with Tom Kat in the lobby when I saw Merry rush in with that dog in tow. She looked harried. When the dog spied Tom Kat, she picked him up. I had vowed to keep my distance. But I felt a jolt of electricity when I saw her. Then the mutt barked.

She left the animal alone again. It doesn't look like there's a man in the picture. Why? Probably one of those women who couldn't be bothered with a real man or who wanted one in a three-piece suit. Never mind. I had my fill of being the knight in shining armor with Patricia. When I traded my suit and tie for jeans and a brown work jacket, and my sports car for a pick-up truck, she went off the deep end. Nothing I did or said could change her mind that owning income property would be better than a company owning me, or us.

For months, I fumed, the disdain on her face imprinted in the back of my mind. With firm resolve, I learned every quirk of the buildings and apartments. An unruly, barking dog could not derail my plans to take ownership of the buildings. Merry and her dog were on my watch list. Unhappy residents were complaining tenants. It's too bad she's so cute, even when she's in a hurry.

Chapter 5

Merry

I called Aunt Liz from work during lunch the next day. Fido had been overcome with excitement when I got in late and I stayed up as long as I could, playing with him, throwing his favorite toy until he settled down.

"Of course, I'll take Fido," Aunt Liz said. "Any time."

"Thank you. I really appreciate this," I said.

"But I have someone I want you to meet," she said.

I groaned. It was a quid pro quo, and I would have to meet another of her matchups. Cautiously, I asked, "Who?" She had trapped me. "Does he like dogs? He isn't allergic, is he?"

"I think he is a pet lover. He doesn't appear to be allergic. And it was not my fault that Sophia failed to tell me her son had allergies." She sniffed.

"I know." I checked the time on my computer and realized the lunch hour was over.

Benjamin waved from his office entry, and I said, "Have to go. We'll chat later." I hung up and started towards him.

"You too," Benjamin motioned towards Kris, and she got up warily. We exchanged curious looks as we walked to Benjamin's office. He gestured toward the chairs facing his desk. While he settled into the high-backed, cushy swivel chair across from us, we eased into the wooden chairs across from him.

"Another company has acquired us. Total Real Estate Management, or TREM," he said. "Have you heard of them?"

"I have," I responded, and looked at Kris.

"Me too." She nodded; her expression was solemn. "They are the biggest owners of commercial real estate in town."

"Yes," he said, his face stoic. "Like any owner, they want to make changes. I wanted to loop you in before I spoke to the rest of the staff. Please keep this news quiet."

"TREM is huge," I said, and asked, "Will there be staffing changes?" My stomach sank at the possibility that I could be back on the job market.

"Yes." He was abrupt and stroked his chin. "But not you two. Your jobs are safe for now." His expression was grim. "The building managers will be consolidated. That is why I am asking you not to divulge what I'm saying to anyone. It will be a challenging period while TREM takes over, evaluates the current operations, and makes the changes they want."

"Sure, boss," Kris said, and nodded.

"No problem," I added. I bit my bottom lip, wanting to ask about Benjamin's position, but I didn't dare.

"What about you?" Kris asked, not as reticent to broach the topic.

"Let me be clear," Benjamin admonished. "No one's job is certain. For now, TREM is not changing my position, data entry, or the office manager. Continue working as you always have. That's it." He nodded dismissively. "Have a good weekend." His head was down while he rustled through papers on his desk as we left.

After the workday, we gathered our belongings and headed out onto the sidewalk with the Friday happy hour crowd in the small town. People were ready to unwind from their week.

"What do you think about the meeting?" Kris asked in a low tone, her full mouth turned down.

"It's not good," I said. "TREM has a reputation for running lean and mean."

"Sharks," Kris agreed, grimly. "I'm getting my resume together this weekend."

"Probably a good idea." I nodded, and we parted ways at the intersection. She headed to her parking place on the side street. Waiting at the corner stoplight on route to my apartment, my mind buzzed with Benjamin's news. A job change would throw another wrench into my carefully ordered life. My job and apartment were at risk, and my school schedule was set. If there were more problems with Joel, I might have to move. I hated change.

I burst inside to Fido's eager licks. We made the trip outdoors and returned to find Joel with Tom Kat perched on his shoulder, lingering by my door.

I held Fido as he strained to get at the cat. Joel gripped Tom Kat.

"Did you want something?" I asked, fearing the worst; another complaint about barking while I was at work.

"Your rent check?" His voice was smooth.

"OMG! Of course!" It was the third of September. It wasn't like me to miss the first of the month's rent payment. Time had escaped me with setting up the new accounts and closing out the books at work. My own finances had suffered. "I'll get a check." I went inside, leaving the door ajar, where Joel waited. He viewed the area while I made out the check with one hand and held Fido firmly with the other.

"Nice job with the kitchen." He nodded approvingly. I had painted the room a mellow shade of yellow and changed out the roller shade for a natural woven material. I had bought a colorful rug that ran the length of the galley-style kitchen. With the fierceness borne of a rejected woman, I had scrubbed the cabinetry and every crook and crevice to the tunes of Adele. Cleaning along to "Rolling in the Deep" had been a catharsis, a renewal from Derrick

Edward Stone's departure, while I had put up an invisible barrier to protect my heart from further hurt.

I had married Derrick with the sounds of wedding bells, in my mind anyway. We had married at the county courthouse with a judge presiding over our vows. It was after finals and before summer school started at the university. After he finished his degree, I discovered Derrick was doing more than studying with his study partner, Sarah.

"Thank you." Mr. and Mrs. Goldman had let me paint and decorate to my taste. I appreciated their philosophy that if the renter made the apartment a home, they were a happy long-term tenant. It was a good policy. In the two months I had lived there, I had met other residents, and a few had lived there for over ten years.

Joel spotted the course book on the kitchen table and asked, "You're studying art?"

"Yes. I take classes at the community college. Art isn't exactly a money-making field." I muttered, "for most people."

"You know, I could use help with the apartments. You have a flair for design." He was thoughtful, gazing around the kitchen.

"Sounds amazing." I relaxed. "Did you want to see the rest of the place?" My eyes locked with his, and I held out my check, still grasping Fido.

"Sure." Joel reached for the check, and I motioned for him to enter. Fido, ever alert, lunged at the black cat, still on the maintenance man's shoulder. The cat raised up on his haunches and hissed. Joel backed off and chuckled. "Another time."

"That's probably best." I smiled and gripped Fido under my arm. Joel's eyes sparkled, and he shut the door.

After the pair left, I hugged Fido and whispered, relieved, "It looks like we won't get kicked out." He licked my face, and I set him down and fed him. My mood was lighter. I felt a warm flush, reliving Joel's compliments about my home and his deep eyes. The possibility of using my passion for art in design was exhilarating. Maybe, Joel wasn't so bad, after all.

Joel

Dang it! Merry was late with the rent. Pacing outside her door, I waited, frustrated like a caged animal. Although she was predictable and I knew she would run in to let the dog out, I hated jumping any tenant about rent. Asking this woman bit. Groaning, I saw her name on the list the Goldman's gave me. Then, cheered by the thought, it was a good excuse to be outside her door. A subtle reminder that her little mutt was trouble and not welcome.

The cheeriness of her place threw me a curve. On the fly, I hatched a plan where I could see her more without the dog. She could redo the apartments, which would make them more marketable. That dog makes me tense. Tom Kat may shed and window peep, but he isn't like the animal that bit me in a flurry when I was a kid. Merry's mutt was a reminder of that time. Then, I loved dogs. Any dog.

It happened on my way to school. While I waited at the bus stop, a neighbor's Pomeranian escaped his house. I was six, a first grader. Impulsively, I ran after it, wanting to capture the fluffy creature. The dog bit me and darted away, his owner in pursuit. I yelped when it bit my hand and then stumbled, hitting the ground with my backpack. Although the bite had not drawn blood, the memory of sharp teeth stayed with me.

Its owner stopped long enough to check my hand, then chased after the animal. The kids on the bus thought it was funny and laughed. The bite hadn't broken the skin and only left a small red mark. Embarrassed by being tackled by a rogue animal in front of a bunch of kids wounded me more. I was wary of dogs now. Fido was as fast as that Pomeranian. I felt humiliated by the kids' jeering and vowed I would never let a dog get that close again.

She looked so happy at the possibility of redesigning apartments; it made my heart sing. Maybe, we could work something out.

Chapter 6

Merry

That night, Aunt Liz called.

"I'll take Fido Thursday after my yoga class. Just bring him over, or I can stop by and get your key," she said. She had recently taken up yoga, and I imagined her balancing on one foot, practicing the 'tree' position as we spoke.

"Fabulous. Thank you so much." Fido was guaranteed to have a quality life with Aunt Liz's fenced-in yard and lavish treats. My penance would be another one of her matches. Sure enough, here it came.

"There is a new fellow I want you to meet," she trilled enthusiastically. "I met him when I was getting the car serviced."

"Oh, boy."

"Now, now," she chided.

"What do you know about him?"

"He's single and appears to be very stable."

"How can you tell?"

"He was getting his Cadillac serviced."

"Oh." Aunt Liz had a Chevy SUV she religiously maintained. A Cadillac was at the high end of the brand.

"I told you, the old-fashioned way of meeting someone would be better than online dating." She chuckled. I could imagine her smug grin and steeled myself.

"So, he has a nice car. What else do you know? He could be a serial killer driving a Cadillac," I countered.

"Don't be silly. I got his address and telephone number."

"You got his address?"

"And I googled."

"You GOOGLED!"

"Do not get your shorts in a bunch, Merry Katherine. I am looking out for you."

"It's okay to snoop online but not to search for a mate online? Through a dating app?"

"Yes. In one instance, you have the information, and you are simply verifying. In the other, that online person can make up an entire portfolio of lies."

"You could still google."

"Never mind," she trilled and gave a hearty laugh. "When do you want to meet Randy?"

"Okay," I said, resigned. "Give him my number."

"Perfect," she chortled and hung up.

After we talked, a flash of Joel's soft blue eyes and his suggestion that I could redo vacancies brought a smile to my face. Then, Joel, as the dog despiser, came to mind. I dismissed all thoughts of Joel with Randy, Aunt Liz's new possibility.

Randy called that evening, and we met at a restaurant near my home the following Saturday afternoon. He was tall, well-muscled, with thinning blond hair, despite being only thirty years old. He arrived promptly at 5:30. With my aunt's vetting, I had opted to meet for appetizers and a drink at his suggestion. My preference was a coffee date during daylight hours. He had been funny and humble during our conversation. It was early for a weekend rendezvous, but if things didn't work out, we both could escape a drawn-out evening. Since I was driving, I wouldn't have more than a glass of wine.

"You must be Merry." He had a slow smile, a deep voice, and a warm presence. He wore casual jeans and a yellow polo shirt under a blue windbreaker.

Aunt Liz may have found a good match.

"Yes. It's nice to meet you." I stuck out my hand. He smiled and took my elbow. "Oh, all right." I folded my arm across my chest as he guided me into the restaurant. We found a reasonably quiet table across from the bar action.

"I love this place. Two-for-one drinks and half-price appetizers before six o'clock. I hope you don't mind?" he asked, with a careful gaze, his chin tucked.

"Sounds good. I am driving, so one glass of wine is my limit," I said.

"No problem. I will have whatever you're having," he said, and he grinned. "But I insist on the loaded nachos."

"I love nachos," I agreed.

We made small talk about our jobs, how often he traveled for work and his love of sports. He was in a softball team for work and enjoyed the camaraderie of the guys. Sports were never my strong suit, and I kept mum while his face glowed about his recent promotion with a major corporation.

I shared my recent trials with work and with having a pet in my apartment building.

"That is rough. A black cat harassing your dog. And a company buyout. You're going through some tough stuff," he said.

"I don't mean to be a downer. Fido keeps me on my toes. You should see the way he barks at Tom Kat." I laughed.

"I'll bet." He snorted. We finished our drinks and the nachos. He scanned the bill. "Let's split this fifty-fifty. I'll get the tip."

"Sure." I flushed and dug out money. Somehow, I thought this would be his treat and was self-conscious about the misunderstanding.

We headed to the exit, and he said, "Your aunt was friendly, and I'm happy she suggested we meet. Could we go to dinner sometime?"

"Okay, just call," I said. Still flustered because he apparently made a comfortable income with a mega corporation but wanted to split the bill. Was I too old-fashioned, like my aunt?

"I'll walk you to your car." His hand on my elbow, we strolled towards our vehicles.

"This is it." I stopped by my blue Ford sedan. Taking my hand, he leaned towards me and brushed his lips against my forehead. I got behind the wheel, cranked the engine, and watched through the rearview mirror as he got into an older pink Cadillac parked a few spaces behind me.

Pink? Really? What was Aunt Liz thinking?

Chapter 7

Merry

When Aunt Liz called Sunday morning, she was exuberant.

"How did it go with Randy?" she asked, breathless.

"Come over, and I'll fill you in."

"Give me an hour."

Fido leaped up and ran to the door when he heard her arrive.

"Oh, he wants a treat," she gushed. Fido jumped around like Snoopy from the Peanuts cartoon, ears flying, eagerly greeting her. She reached into her pocket. "Here you go."

"Yep, he knows a mark when he sees one," I said, laughing at his antics. "Oh, before I forget, I'll give you a key so you can get him when it's convenient on Thursday." I dug into my bag and got a spare and put the purse aside.

"Thanks." She pocketed it. "So, how is it going with the black cat?" We settled on the couch in my small living room, hot mugs of coffee in hand.

"We haven't been evicted yet. The last time Fido and Tom Kat saw each other was at a safe distance. Joel was waiting for me at my door with the cat riding his shoulder. I had forgotten to pay the rent."

"That doesn't sound like you." She frowned.

"It isn't. Or at least, I hope it's not what I'm turning into. Forgetful, with a ferocious dog ready to charge." We both chuckled at the sight of Fido, now sprawled at my feet.

"So, tell me." Aunt Liz's eyes sparkled. "How did it go with Randy?"

"Umm. He is interesting." I brushed a lock of hair back, avoiding her inquisitive gaze. I didn't want to disappoint her. Randy was attractive and had potential, but his spending habits, or lack of spending on our first encounter, were off-putting.

"Whenever someone says it's interesting, it means not so good." She probed my expression. "Let's hear it."

"We met for happy hour at El Toro."

"Perfect. They have those great nachos, and two-for-one drinks. Low commitment, casual," she said.

"You know the place?" I viewed her, surprised that she was familiar with a sports bar that was commonly known for singles. Fine dining, white tablecloths, and cloth napkins were more her style.

"I get out." She fluffed her hair and looked away, a smirk lingering. "Go on."

"Maybe I misunderstood. I thought it was his treat because he suggested the place." I was sheepish. "We split the bill. He left the tip."

"He didn't pay?" She gasped. "In my day, that was a deal breaker."

"Well, things are different now. Women don't assume the man will pay."

"Oh, poo. He isn't financially strapped, is he? He appeared stable."

"I think he is well set. He said he recently got a promotion, and he works for a major corporation." I shrugged, and asked, frowning, "You didn't say he drove an older model car? Pink."

"Yes. It is a collector. It is beautiful." She gushed. "From the 90s, I believe."

"Uh, huh." I nodded. It was a great-looking car, but a boat by today's standards. A car suitable for a vintage car show, not one you'd drive every day.

"Okay." She leaned into the cushions and stroked her chin, "So we know he wouldn't blow the budget. He is careful with his money. It would have been better if he had paid the bill, but this was a trial run. Check each other out. That was the idea, right?" She brightened.

"Yes. He said he wanted to go to dinner," I conceded. "He said he'd call."

"So, give him another chance. But take money with you, just in case." She snickered. "He might be a solid match if he is conservative with money. Planning for the possibility of supporting a family?" She patted my knee. "We will find you the right man. I promise."

"Sure, Aunt Liz."

"Now, that's the right attitude. How are things at work?" she asked with a cheerful smile.

"Oh," I groaned. "That's another story. The company is being bought out by TREM. Total Real Estate Management."

"Oh dear. They will want to make changes." She sighed. "Job consolidation and all of that. Have they told you how that affects your position?"

"Benjamin said they were making changes with the building managers. Not as much with office staff. I'm safe for now."

"Okay, dearie." She checked her watch. "I must go. I'm meeting one of the knitters for lunch." She got up, smoothing her slacks.

"Sophia?"

"Goodness, no. I don't know what to say to her, considering how she misled me about her son. Allergies, indeed." She huffed and took her cup to the kitchen. I followed, leaving my mug on the counter. "You've done wonders with this place, Merry." She gazed with a satisfied smile. "It is quite comfortable. The yellow color is so warm."

"Thank you." I flushed at her compliment.

She reached for me, and a whiff of her favorite perfume greeted me. We hugged. "I'll be over Thursday to get this little guy." She reached down to stroke Fido's head. As I closed the door behind her, farther down the hall, I heard her lilting voice. "Hello. That is a beautiful cat you have there."

Joel's voice came. "Thanks. He's a great companion."

Fido sniffed excitedly at the crack under the door, giving a little yip and then a growl.

"That's it, mister. No problems today," I warned. I slipped into sneakers and leashed him. "We're going to work off some of that energy." We headed out to the dog park two blocks from the building, where he ran free, meeting and nosing a Bichon Frise. The park was next to the river walk, and people were out enjoying the late summer, hiking the walkway. There was a canoe rental place and an ice cream stand. The sun was warm, and I forgot my worries about work, men, and home as I watched the dog's play.

"Merry!"

I heard the man's voice and turned to face him. "Randy!"

He waved and ran from the river's path towards the dog area. His tee-shirt clung to his chest, wet with perspiration. Blue jogging shorts showed tanned legs. He stopped beside me and put one hand on the wire fence, the other on his muscular thigh, while he caught his breath.

"I didn't know you ran here," I said.

Regaining his breath, and surveying the dog area, he said, "Yes. I get over here as often as possible. So, this is where you and your dog hang out?"

"As often as we can," I echoed his words.

"It's a fun place," he said and nodded. Fido saw Randy beside me, and he ditched the Bichon and ran to the fence. Stopping, he put his nose through the wire and sniffed Randy's leg. "Hey, buddy." Kneeling, he reached through the wire to pet him and was rewarded with a nip, then withdrew his hand and shook it. "He bit me!"

"Fido!" I scolded. "Let me see." I examined his hand. The skin was red where the dog had seized his finger. "I'm sorry. He is very protective."

"It's okay." Randy viewed his hand and rubbed it. "No blood." He chuckled cautiously. He glanced over at me, then at Fido. "Well, you guys enjoy the park. See you." He started off at a trot and gained momentum as he ran onto the path by the lake.

Great. Now my dog was biting any man who got near me. "No biting," I admonished, and leashed him. He gazed at me with solemn eyes. I relented. "You were only protecting me." I stroked his fur and headed home.

Joel

The woman who visits Merry is super friendly. Must be a relative. They look alike, with longish, honey-brown hair and streaks of blonde. Plus, she likes Tom Kat. Anyone who likes cats can't be bad. After she left, I saw Merry go out with that little mutt leading the way. I had been on the side lawn, picking up litter. Her blue denim jacket is sharp, and those jeans hugged her frame. Super cute.

It was a perfect day for a walk, and on the spur of the moment, I thought, why not? The lawn could wait. I left Tom Kat lounging on the couch at my place and headed toward the river walk. The sun was warm while I strolled, and I kept my distance from the pair. I was about to approach Merry at the dog park a safe distance from the mutt, when a jogger in front of me ran up to her. Puzzled, I hung back, found an empty bench, and watched covertly. I wasn't sure why I found her so interesting. She was refreshing, and dang it, devoted to that dog. Her commitment was attractive. Am I becoming a stalker?

The jogger offered his hand to the dog and then jerked it back. I snickered. Fido bit him. Maybe the mutt was smarter than I give him credit. He hadn't bitten me. The man ran off, and I watched Merry scold the animal. At least she is trying to keep him in line. I felt something stir inside for this woman that I hadn't felt for a long while. What the heck was I going to do about this gorgeous woman with the beautiful smile and her plucky attitude?

Chapter 8

Merry

"Fido was warning Randy," Kris said at work the next day, holding back a snicker, then serious. "Dogs can sense who's a good person and who isn't."

"Biting is serious. He cannot bite anyone," I protested. "Not even a bad person."

"Huh?" She frowned.

"Well, maybe a bad person, but only if I say so," I amended.

"You'll have to get a muzzle," she said. "Just to be safe. You don't want him to bite a kid or anything. Get some dog training."

"Yes. I will get a muzzle."

Along with filling her in about Randy at the dog park, we talked about our meeting at the restaurant, and she was quick to side with me. "Did he tip on the whole bill?"

"I don't know."

"You're supposed to tip on the entire bill. It is the right thing to do." She folded her arms across her generous chest and lowered her chin, meeting my gaze.

"I agree." I nodded.

"You don't have to decide about him right away." She studied me. "If something doesn't feel right, pay attention to that creepy feeling."

"Okay." I considered Kris's advice. "Good idea. Especially after Derrick." I had dismissed any queasy feeling, then discovered he had already moved on with a newly minted degree.

"Your aunt wants to find the best match for you," she counseled. "That's not a bad thing."

"It isn't, and she does." I laughed.

"The old-fashioned way," Kris added.

"Yes." I nodded.

"Nowadays, people meet through dating sites."

"That's how I met Derrick," I countered. "You know how well that worked out."

"Dating sites were new then. They were the wild west of dating."

"Yeah. Derrick was the wild west, all right," I muttered.

"Don't dismiss them altogether. It is another way to meet new people. It will put you in the zone." She raised her brows and studied me.

"The zone?"

"It means you are open to meeting someone. The more prospects you meet, the more signals you send that you are interested in finding your Mr. Right. It's like job hunting."

I groaned.

"And your aunt can still try to find a match for you the old-fashioned way." She shrugged.

"That's true."

"We'll set up a profile for you." She beamed. "It'll be fun."

"Oh, boy." I gulped.

About then, Benjamin came out of his office and said, "Kris, Merry," and waved us over.

"Now what?" Kris muttered. We exchanged grimaces and went into his office.

We perched on the edge of the hard chairs as Benjamin shut the door, then eased into his cushy desk chair. He leaned back, clasped his hands on his chest, and stared. Peering over his glasses, he said, "TREM has decided to go in another direction. They are going to close this office and merge operations with another office's staff."

"When?" I sat stunned. Kris's rosy complexion paled. She flinched, and her frames slipped.

"We will move the office by November 1. That will give us time to notify all the accounts of the change in ownership. Okay?" He added, "We'll need help with the move."

"Of course." Kris and I nodded.

"Do you have any questions?" He was brisk as he glanced at folders on his desk.

"So, we're going to the new office?" I held my breath, waiting for his response.

"Yes."

Kris and I exhaled, relieved. At least we had jobs until November.

"That is all for now. Please keep our conversations confidential." He flipped over a manilla file and looked over at us with a small sly smile.

"Of course!" we answered in unison and left his office.

On our way to our desks, I whispered, "I don't like this. Benjamin is being cagey."

"Me, either. I hate change." The corners of Kris's mouth turned down.

"Do you think TREM is going to fire us?" I whispered.

"Don't know, but I'm nearly finished updating my resume. You should too." She matched my low voice.

"Benjamin says no," I said, trying to be optimistic. "We're going to the new office."

"TREM might get rid of Benjamin," Kris suggested. "Maybe that's why he's so tense."

"Yeah, they could." I nodded and signed into my computer.

"Let's get together and get your profile done," Kris said. "We need a diversion while we work on our resumes."

"Sure." I grimaced. "How about this Friday after work?" I asked. "At my place."

"Perfect. We can get takeout, make it a party." Kris's good humor returned, and we settled in to finish our workday.

The next few days were a blur until Thursday night's Art and Design class. Aunt Liz called to tell me she had picked up Fido after her yoga session.

"How was he?" I asked, concerned. He had never had company while I was gone.

"He was delightful. I cannot believe he bit anyone. He was sleeping and went into doggy delight when I came in. He was so excited." She chuckled as she related Fido's antics. "I ran into that building manager of yours too, with the cat riding his shoulder. That cat has him wrapped around his paws."

"You didn't have Fido with you?"

"No."

"Great. No drama," I said, relieved.

"When will you pick him up?" she asked.

"Class is out at nine. I'll be at your house about nine-thirty."

"We'll see you then."

"Thanks. I appreciate this." I had disconnected from her when my cell phone sounded again. Wincing, I read the caller's name. It was Randy.

"Glad I caught you," he said. "I hope we can do dinner tomorrow night."

"Sorry. I am busy then." I thought guiltily of Kris's plan to make a dating profile and work on our resumes.

"Saturday night then?"

"That works." I was surprised that he called, considering the incident at the park on Sunday.

"Seven o'clock?" he added wryly, "I'll bring a treat for the dog. Text me your address."

"Sure." I hung up, sent the text, and looked over at Kris, who wore a big grin.

"That was Randy?" she asked, batting her lashes.

"Yes. We're going out Saturday."

"He couldn't be too upset about Fido."

"Thank goodness. No."

"We'll see what Fido does," she said. "We're still on for Friday?"

"Yes."

"See, the zone is already working." She was smug. "It'll be magical, and we'll find your mate in no time."

"Good grief." I laughed, flushing at the idea.

***

Friday night, over pizza and light beer, Kris and I giggled at the profile questions on the site she chose.

"What are you passionate about?" Kris asked and snickered.

"My dog," I said, stoic.

"Probably not what a man wants," she said. Her eyes sparkled.

"It is if he's equally passionate about his dog," I said firmly.

"I think there may be an issue if you are looking for a soul mate." She giggled again. "A human male."

"Whatever." I shrugged.

"Let's try the next question. 'What do you enjoy doing in your leisure time?'"

"Spending quality time with my dog, throwing his toy, going for walks."

"So, long walks along the river path in the moonlight," she suggested.

I frowned.

"What? Show *some* interest in romance or bonding," she said. Seeing my worried expression, "We should eat." She closed the website, and we grabbed a slice of pepperoni pizza.

"Tell me about the dude with the cat," she demanded after a bite of food.

"His name is Joel, and he's the building manager," I said. "He is impossible, and I stay far, far away from him. The man does not like dogs, and I cannot stand the sight of him. You saw him?" My nose wrinkled.

"Yes, on the way in. He's cute. Especially with that cat." She giggled.

"Harrumph. Not that cute. You should see how that cat eyes Fido." I put my arm around my dog, comforting him. "He menaces him."

"You can't confuse the man with the cat's temperament," she said. "Doesn't Joel remind you of someone, a movie star?" Her face scrunched as she thought.

"Liam Hemsley, without the Aussie accent."

"Ooh! That's it." She chortled. "He's a hunk."

"He is sort of cute." My brows furrowed, and I shrugged, recalling his dimpled smile and calm presence.

"But you've got a date with Mr. Pink Cadillac tomorrow." Her eyebrows rose.

"Randy." I laughed. "It should be interesting. Fido has him on his bite list." Stroking the dog, I studied him. "Promise me you won't bite."

Chapter 9

Merry

Randy knocked promptly at seven, and Fido went into high alert mode. I tucked him under my arm and greeted Randy. He wore casual pants, a buttoned-down collar shirt, and a black fleece jacket for the cool late September evening. He looked freshly scrubbed and held out a milk bone. Fido never lost a beat, indeed barking louder at his gesture.

"Sorry." I shrugged. "I'll put him in his kennel." I headed to the bedroom, where Fido's rarely used crate was stored. Sometimes, it calmed him down. Tucking him away, I gave him a snack. He whimpered, and I whispered, "It's okay. I'll be back soon." After a brief whine, he settled down, munching his treat. I closed the door. Randy stood in the hall by the exit, waiting.

He joked. "Shall we make a run for it?"

"We should." I nodded, collected my purse from the coffee table, and grabbed my jacket. There was another whine from the bedroom as we left. We relaxed, walking into the night air amid the sounds of the traffic and felt the cool breeze.

"That was close." Randy chuckled. "He heard us leave. It could have been a full-on bark fest."

"He's very protective."

"That's good." He looked approving, and we got into the vintage Cadillac.

"Is this a collector car?" I fastened the seat belt.

"Yes. It was my mother's. She made a lot of money selling cosmetics. When the lease was up, she bought it. She loved this car."

"Mary Kay?"

"No. Different company. Her company had the bright, hot pink. Mary Kay cars are lighter, almost salmon colored."

"Good for her. I'm impressed."

"After she retired, she gave me the car. It was a great deal."

"Uh, huh."

"Do you like Italian food?" he asked.

"I do. Spaghetti, lasagna, pizza; all of it." I smiled.

"Good, that's where we'll go." Randy drove the car at a steady speed to a restaurant in an out of the way strip mall.

The restaurant was part of a chain known for casual dining. The décor was bright and colorful, and it was modestly busy on a Saturday evening. We were seated in a high-backed wooden booth.

"This works for tonight?" Randy waved a coupon at the hostess.

"Yes."

Randy looked at me. "It's a buy one, get one deal. It's good for an entrée up to $20."

For a moment, I was speechless and considered an exit plan. Then I calmed down. I was on a budget too and would try to be reasonable. There were worse things than a coupon. Aunt Liz could be right. He was planning for a time when he would have a family to provide for. Everybody has quirks. I had Fido.

"Sure. I will have the lasagna."

"Make that two," Randy said.

"Anything to drink?" the server asked.

"A diet cola," I said, avoiding Randy's gaze.

"Me, too." After the server left, he said, "The coupon calls for two beverages," and put it aside.

Ah, that explains why he would spring for two drinks.

We made polite conversation while we waited for our entrees. Randy talked about his softball team and his next trip for work. He was charming and chatty, and I felt myself relaxing. At the end of the evening, he drove me home, and we walked to my door.

"Thank you for dinner," I said. We heard barking from the kennel in the bedroom. I gestured toward the doorknob. "I'd better go in," and stuck out my hand. He grasped it and leaned in to kiss my cheek.

"This was fun." He was jovial. He straightened and headed to the staircase.

"Sure." I breathed a sigh of relief at his parting back and darted inside.

* * *

"He used a COUPON?" Kris exclaimed on break Monday morning at work. She leaned back in her chair and faced me.

"Yep," I said, my face flushed. "He must be on a budget," I added, defensively.

"I don't like it." She shook her head. "That means he's taking out a lot of women or he's cheap. He offered to take you to dinner. And he has a job?"

"Yes. He has a great job." I shrugged. "He talked about all the fancy places he stays in while he travels for his company."

"He paid for drinks?"

"Yes, the coupon asked for two beverages."

"And he picked you up?"

"He did." I nodded.

"How did he tip?"

"On one entrée and two drinks." I had paid attention and mentally calculated how much he had spent against the tip he left.

"Harrumph. Do you like him?"

"He seems nice, and he's pretty humble," I admitted. "He wasn't arrogant about his job." I tilted my head. "He was confident about his work. He is cute, in a thinning hair sort of way."

"Okay." She relaxed. "Well, give him more time, but a man who is cheap with money is cheap with his love. He could just as well go out by himself with a coupon and get the second entrée to go. You're helping him out."

"How?" I asked, puzzled.

"By ordering that second beverage." We dissolved into peals of laughter. I sobered up and said, "Aunt Liz says he may be frugal because he's thinking about the future and the possibility of supporting a family."

She let out another harrumph.

"He has to snag you first. Lavish time and spend some money. That's what I think." She arched her brows. "We need to get back to that dating profile."

"Uh, huh?" I feigned a yawn and turned to my computer. "I need to get this report done. Benjamin wanted an update for Mr. Bigg."

Kris focused on her computer screen. I considered her opinion of the two-for-one deals, a cheap man, and love. I felt funny about the coupons with Randy. He had been pleasant company, but she had a point. If I were in a long-term relationship with him, coupons wouldn't be a problem. We just didn't know each other that well. But I still wasn't thrilled about meeting people through a dating site.

"Merry and Kris!" Benjamin waved from his doorway. He hovered, his broad frame imposing as we filed past him into his office, closing the door. After we sat, shifting uneasily, he said, "TREM is investing heavily in the town of Reindeer Falls. They want the staff to get involved too. Advertising for the holidays starts early, and he wants us to brainstorm holiday decorations for the annual Reindeer Days Festival. I want you two to come up with ideas for them before we move to the office. The earlier, the better."

"Sounds like fun," I said and looked over at Kris, who was busy examining her nails.

"I'm more of a participant than a presenter," she demurred.

"Uh huh." Benjamin leaned back in his chair and steepled his hands. With a firm voice and a cunning smile, he said, "Maybe you can dig deep, find an idea that says Reindeer is the place to celebrate the season. There is a ten-thousand-dollar cash prize to the winner."

My eyes were wide, startled. "I can do that. No problem. We'll make a plan," I said, glancing at Kris.

"We will meet, say, in two weeks. Mid-October." He scanned his calendar. "I look forward to your ideas. Then we'll start packing up the office the following week and move the week after."

Kris and I huddled at my desk after the meeting.

"Why were you so negative, Kris? Our jobs are on the line," I whispered.

"I think we're toast, anyway. He wants to steal our ideas and run with them to TREM, to save his behind," she retorted.

"Oh dear. Why do you say that?" I asked, my shoulders tense.

"You don't know Benjamin like I know him," she said sagely.

"Huh?" That was true. Kris had worked at the company for a year when I applied.

"The clerk before you found some discrepancies in the accounts," she whispered. "She asked Benjamin about them, and she was out by the day's end."

"No!" I was horrified.

"Yep." She was grim.

"What discrepancies?" I had seen nothing amiss, but I didn't handle the important accounts like Mr. Bigg's.

"I'm not sure. I called the woman, but she told me that when Benjamin fired her, he warned her that if she talked to anyone from the company, he would not pay severance. She had to sign an NDA, a non-disclosure agreement."

"So, why was she fired?" I frowned.

"The official reason was company downsizing, just like now." She hesitated, adding. "But then he hired you."

"Oh, great." They had hired me on a lie. I groaned. "But you're still here."

"I kept mum. I need this job."

"Merry!" Benjamin towered over my desk. Kris's face turned a bright shade of red, and she darted back to her station.

"Yes?" I stood up, flustered.

"Until we move, any bills you get in the mail, give them to me."

"Okay." My face matched the color of Kris's.

"It'll give you more time to brainstorm for the holiday festival."

"Sure." That was the one bright light on the horizon. I already had an idea for TREM's participation. But what if the project was just a ruse to look good to TREM's management and fire me? My stomach churned at the prospect.

I caught up with Kris on the sidewalk after work. "Do you have any idea what Benjamin was doing with the accounts?" We stood face to face, shoulders hunched.

She clutched her scarf, and her bright eyes met mine.

"I don't know for sure. My guess is that he was writing checks from trust accounts. Business was down, rentals were slow, bills were due."

"An audit would catch that."

"Yep, and that's when he blamed the bookkeeper. After the company audit."

"But I haven't seen anything out of the ordinary. He wouldn't have any reason to fire me."

"Would you know?" she asked. Her mouth twitched.

"You mean, would I know if he was writing checks from the wrong accounts?"

"Yes." She studied me.

"No," I conceded. "He keeps the trust accounts in his office."

She stared at me.

"That's it, isn't it? He wrote checks from the trust accounts where the damage deposits are held until the tenant moves!" I exclaimed. That was strictly taboo, writing checks from trust accounts to cover other bills. A person could be held personally liable for the mismanaged money.

"That's my guess. The bookkeeper would not say for sure. So, I cannot confirm, nor deny, that statement," Kris said, her lips pressed. Burrowing into her jacket, she wrapped her scarf around her neck as if she felt a cold chill.

"I won't ask you to." I flinched, shrugged deeper into my coat, and we parted ways at the corner stoplight.

Chapter 10

Merry

I ENTERED MY BUILDING and dug out my mailbox key in a funk, mulling over my conversation with Kris. Flipping through the mail while sorting advertising from bills, the door opened behind me.

"You look like you've had a bad day," Joel commented as he breezed into the lobby. Without Tom Kat perched on his shoulder, he was strikingly handsome with an engaging smile and eyes that lit up when he saw me. At least, I thought they did.

"It's just work." I wasn't going to unload on the building super. "Where is your sidekick? Tom Kat?" I motioned towards his usual perch.

"Gave him the day off." His voice was smooth and held a hint of laughter.

"You mean he's chasing mice?" I teased. "Or window peeping?"

"Probably." He laughed. It was a relief to banter. The air was warm, and Joel was easy to talk to. He nodded.

"That looks like the Reindeer Holiday Festival flyer you're holding."

"This soon?" I exclaimed.

"Yes. People in Reindeer take their holidays seriously," he said soberly. He tipped his head and smiled.

"So I've heard." I nodded. I was grim.

"Is something wrong?" He looked at me curiously.

"My company wants me and Kris, the office manager, to come up with ideas for our new owner to take part in the festival."

"Great!"

"Yes. It will be fun. It seems early." I glanced at the flyer. "It isn't even Halloween."

"Comes earlier every year," he asserted.

"Well, Fido probably has all fours crossed." Shrugging, clutching the mail and flyers, I went toward the staircase. His steps sounded behind me. Wincing, I heard yipping from behind my door. Joel's footfalls continued up to the third floor. I flew inside, greeted the dog, and hushed him at the same time.

"We don't want to cause a disturbance, now, do we?" I said to the eager little dog. Scooping him up and securing him, we went outside.

Dried leaves littered the street and the pet area. A cool wind whipped between the buildings. October could bring snow, but I hoped for a long late summer. I waited while Fido did his business, then dug in my pocket for a baggie. "Oh nuts, no baggie." I would have to come back. We trekked inside. In the flurry of grabbing the refuse baggie, the phone rang.

"Merry. How did your dinner date with Randy go?" Aunt Liz's voice was high and breathless. "I've been waiting for an update."

"It was interesting."

"Again, what happened?" Aunt Liz demanded.

"It's nothing." I hated to dim her enthusiasm.

"What is it?" she asked, exasperated.

"Randy seems nice, but he had a coupon for dinner." I flushed, feeling uneasy. "Coupons are for committed couples. Don't you think?"

"I see. It *is* quirky. Maybe he's paying bills for an elderly parent or something?"

A loud knock sounded at the entry. Checking the peephole, I said, "I have to go. The maintenance man is here. I will call you later."

"Oh, is it that cute fellow with the adorable cat?" she trilled as I hung up. I opened the door to a sober-faced Joel.

"What is it?" I asked.

"I have to give you this." He shoved a piece of paper at me. "It's the warning I told you about. All tenants must pick up their animal waste."

"But I was just going back," I said, and waved the baggie.

"Sorry, company policy. I can't read your mind." He shuffled awkwardly, then backed away.

"But, but..." I sputtered as he turned and walked down the hallway. "What a jerk!" I closed the door.

I speed dialed Aunt Liz, my face hot with anger. "The dude just wrote me up for littering! The nerve. He had to have been watching."

"Littering?" she asked.

"I forgot a baggie for Fido," I explained, whining, "I was going back, honest."

"Don't be too hard on him. He must be firm or things get out of hand. How often has this happened?"

"This is my first written warning. Three, and I'm out." I sighed.

"It won't happen again, Merry. Just forget about it and don't let it bother you. What fun things do you have planned for the week?"

I crumpled up the warning paper and tossed it. "Just my class. But I have orders from Benjamin to work up suggestions for the Reindeer Holiday Festival."

"Perfect! It starts the day after Halloween, right?"

"Yes."

"They have the lighting, baking, and the decorating contest?"

"Uh huh, and more. TREM wants to get involved with the festivities to generate goodwill for their massive expansion into buying apartment buildings."

"Excellent idea. It sounds like they are going to dominate the rental market in town," she said. "It could be a good thing for Reindeer Falls if they provide housing at a reasonable price."

"TREM isn't known for affordable housing."

"That's not good," she mused.

"That's what companies are all about—more profit, less service."

"You *are* on a downer. Is something else wrong?"

"It's nothing. I've had better days, that's all." I did not want to burden Aunt Liz with the gossip about Benjamin. Kris could have her facts wrong.

"Hold on, there is a call coming in." I frowned at the Caller ID. Randy, already? "It's Randy," I said.

"I'll let you go," she breezed. "I have another yoga class tonight." She hung up.

"Hello?"

"Merry, I am having pizza tonight. How would you and Fido like to come over? We could walk before or after." He was cheerful, and I was pleased he had included my pet.

"That sounds great. No pizza for Fido. I'll bring his chow."

"Of course." He was upbeat.

"Is a half-hour, okay? I need to change. I just got in from work."

"That's good. We can have a short walk while the food is in the oven." Hesitating, he added, "Uh, I've been working on the place. It's a work-in-process, a fixer-upper." He chuckled.

"How bad can it be?" I teased. "You are cooking?"

I threw on jeans and a hoodie, leashed Fido, and headed towards Randy's house.

Four blocks over, I stood in front of the residence, matching the house with the number Randy had given me, puzzled. It looked abandoned, except for the pink Cadillac parked in the narrow drive. The bushes at the entry were scraggly and overgrown. Paint was chipped and worn on the siding. Cobwebs clung to the corners of the entrance and the sidewalk was littered with cracks. He threw open the door, wearing a ragged sweatshirt and jeans.

"Great timing. I just put in the pizza. We'll have about twenty minutes to work up an appetite."

"Sounds good."

Shutting his door, he checked his watch, and we headed to the river path.

After a few steps, I asked, "So, you're fixing up the house?"

"Yep. Bought it two years ago. The plan is to live downstairs and rent out the upstairs."

"Nice!" Was that why he was thrifty, fixing up his home?

"I'll need to find a renter." He gave me a sideways glance. "Someone who doesn't mind a little construction dust." He grinned.

"Uh, huh?" I glanced at him, uncertain. "You've owned it for two years?"

"Yep. With work and travel, I haven't done as much as I would like." He grimaced.

"Sure. It takes time to renovate." I nodded.

We circled back to the duplex for dinner after a few minutes of walking, admiring the red and gold foliage of the fall, enjoying the change of season.

Sniffing the air appreciatively, we entered the house. The kitchen was on the left, and I paused, surveying the area. There was dust everywhere. Worn faded curtains hung limply at the window over the kitchen sink, where dishes left from earlier meals sat waiting to be washed. Randy hurried to the oven. I squinted, seeing burners crusted with leftovers. He reached into the caked-on, burned food oven, and took out a pizza. The box from the store brand pizza was in the garbage can next to the stove. The kitchen table was cleared for two paper plates. At one end, there was a stack of file folders and a laptop computer. My appetite was gone.

"OMG!" Slapping the side of my head, I said, "I forgot about Aunt Liz's club night! I must go!" I blurted out the first thing that came to mind. Okay, I didn't exactly lie—I didn't say I was going to the knitting club, or that it was that night. The inference was the lie.

Fido tugged his leash toward the exit.

"I am so sorry. It was silly of me to forget."

"If you're sure." He looked bewildered, and for a moment, I felt sorry for him. Then, I thought of all the germs that had to be fermenting in the kitchen. "My company has scheduled me for out-of-town travel next week. It is a shame we won't see each other."

I apologized again and left red-faced.

When Fido whined, I reassured him, "We will eat soon. At least we got in our walk." I hiked home, stomach growling, the sidewalk a blur, and my thoughts in a whirl. I came out of my trance when I entered my building and groaned. It was Joel again, this time with Tom Kat, lounging by the security phone. Why was he here? Was he spying, looking for some infraction to give me another warning?

My shoulders stiffened, and I tried to ignore him.

"Merry," he said, his blue eyes twinkling. "I want to apologize for earlier."

"Okay." I relented. He looked like he was sorry.

"I had to warn you about Fido. I did not have to be so harsh." His tone was soothing.

"Apology accepted." Although the warning still stung. Tom Kat perched on Joel's shoulder, burrowing into his neck, his eyes bright, still vigilant.

Fido blinked and watched the pair, alert.

"Thank you for apologizing." I shrugged. "We have to go." We passed the two, and Fido bounded up the steps, taking the lead. "At least you didn't bark," I muttered. Grinning, I entered my place, pleased that at least one thing had gone well that day. Raising the shade and window in the kitchen, to air out the room, I busied myself getting dog chow and rifled through the refrigerator and cupboards for my dinner. Spotting an emergency can of clam chowder, I said, "Excellent." Then, I heated the food and ate with gusto. With every bite, the frustrations of the day faded, and the image of Joel apologizing warmed me.

Joel

I came down hard by giving a written warning, but I have to keep on top of the maintenance, otherwise people won't want to live here. The apartment business is tough, and Holly Street's reputation was top-notch. I can feel TREM bearing down on Reindeer Falls, like every other small apartment owner. They want to trample decent owners by luring tenants with free rent, then trap them by raising rates, and/or cut back on services, so profits meant more than quality. A barking dog could drive a renter who may be on the edge into one of TREM's buildings.

She looked devastated when I shoved the paper at her, and I felt guilty. There was a spark, too. Animal attraction. She wore that danged cute jean jacket again, and her tousled hair fell in waves around her face. I *love* the windblown look. She looked distracted, giving her an air of innocence.

I missed seeing her the last few days. When she burst into the lobby, I surprised her, and she looked wary. Thank goodness that mutt didn't bark or lunge at Tom Kat. When I apologized, her sweet smile warmed me. It's a start to a more cordial relationship, and maybe more?

Chapter 11

Merry

I CALLED AUNT LIZ over lunchtime from work the next day and described Randy's house.

"The place needs a woman's touch," Aunt Liz cooed.

"Along with the woman's rent money," I retorted.

"He didn't say that, did he?" She gasped.

"Sort of," I admitted. "That seemed to be the general drift."

"We will keep working on it. Maybe Randy isn't right for you. Was there any spark at all?" she asked, with a wisp of regret in her voice.

I thought about the layer of dust and neglect in his place.

"Just the potential spark that could set that place of his on fire."

"Oh, dear." She laughed. "Let's get together and plan something for the festival. It will be fun."

"This weekend would work."

"Fine. I will get Fido on Thursday. We enjoy our afternoons together." She chuckled again.

"Thank you. I'll pick him up after class, and I appreciate it." Fido was calmer when he saw Tom Kat the last time, but I did not want to take any chances. Especially after Joel's warning.

I hung up from Aunt Liz as Kris breezed in from lunch, hung up her coat, and settled in at her desk. I filled her in on the prior evening's events.

"Gross," she said, adding a throaty laugh. "I think I've seen that car around the neighborhood." She wrinkled her nose. "It's pink, bright pink."

"Yes, it is." My brows rose.

"We need to finish your profile." At my grimace, she added, "It's a good way to get out and meet people. Even if it doesn't lead to Mr. Right."

"The zone thing." I groaned. "Any thoughts on the festival?"

"Not yet, but did you hear about the building owner who buys properties, raises the rents, and doesn't make repairs or pay for garbage removal or maintenance?"

"No. Who is that?"

"Not sure, but," she said, "he has a silent partner." She sent me a conspiratorial glance, and rolled her chair to my desk, and whispered, "I think his partner is Mr. Bigg."

"No!"

"Merry, Kris!" Hearing Benjamin's command from his office, we stood and responded, "Yes!" in unison. We glanced at each other; eyebrows raised. Kris's glasses slipped down the bridge of her nose, and she jabbed them up.

"In here!" He motioned us into his office.

We sat gingerly, inhaling, while he closed the door and sat across from us at his desk.

"TREM, our new owner, wants both of you to list your duties and the time each duty takes. Of course, this is only a planning exercise and in no way affects your positions. They intend to take both of you to their new offices."

"Uh, huh." I glanced at Kris, where she focused on Benjamin.

"The next few days, I'd like each of you to give me your list on Friday, before you leave for the weekend."

"Sure, boss." Kris sounded upbeat.

"Of course," I chimed.

"That'll be all." Benjamin looked over at us with a sly smile and, with a short wave, dismissed us.

We went back to our desks.

"OMG!" I whispered. "What do you think?"

"I'm glad my resume is done." She matched my tone. "How about you?"

"It's on the list," I said glumly.

"Don't worry," she continued in a hushed voice. "They need us to pack up the office and move. And they want our ideas for the town's festival. Besides, if they fire us, we'll just get new jobs. Better jobs!"

"Right!" I took out a yellow legal pad from my desk drawer and started listing each duty, my stomach tied in knots.

For the next few days, I jotted down my responsibilities and the time to perform, per Benjamin's request. At night, I updated my resume. It was a relief to go to class Thursday night and focus on design. Reflecting on how awesome it would be to create beautiful new spaces; I recalled the visiting artist's cautions earlier in the term: "My occupation is the reason I am not married." He added that "commissioned art projects were few, and far between." Not a resounding motive for an art degree. It would have to be an avocation, not a vocation.

Aunt Liz had picked Fido up that afternoon. When I collected him after class later that night, she gushed. "He's such a good boy!" She sent a new toy. Dressed in her fuzzy pink robe and matching slippers, she was ready for bed.

"Thanks, Aunt Liz. We will talk tomorrow." We left; the stuffed toy clenched in Fido's mouth.

***

Benjamin came to our desks Friday afternoon and collected our lists. Kris and I walked out of the office, exchanging grim looks.

"I told Benjamin that Mr. Cratchit or Scrooge would be a good theme for TREM," she said with a smirk. We paused on the sidewalk.

"That would fit with the company mission." I snickered.

"You bet it would," she retorted with a head toss.

"He didn't like the idea?" I asked with a chuckle.

"He is so arrogant. I don't think he got the message!" She snickered, and we parted ways.

I breezed into my apartment, hearing Fido's excited barks echoing through the hall. Gasping, I dashed to the kitchen window and looked out. Tom Kat sat on the fire escape, licking his paws. Distracted by my closing the window shade, he stopped, glared, and hunched his back, ready to leap. He changed his mind and sat again, as if he were sure I was no threat. The cat was right. Then there was a sharp rap at the door.

It was Joel. He met my gaze through the security hole, waiting while I opened the door.

"Hate to do this, Merry." He shoved a piece of paper at me. It was another warning. He shrugged. "Someone complained about your dog barking."

"It was your cat that started it!" I protested. Snatching the paper and shutting the door in his face. Wearily, I changed into jeans and a hoodie, took Fido out, then returned to feed him, and made a quick dinner of tomato soup. Supplies were getting slim. Groceries were a must do that weekend.

"What time should we get together tomorrow?" Aunt Liz's call was a welcome distraction. Her voice cheered me. "How about noon? I'll get us lunch on the way over?"

"Great idea," I said. I finished my soup. With plans made for the next day, I headed out for a walk with Fido.

We trotted down to the first floor, where tenants were moving out. I heard the commotion of furniture and a couple emerged from an apartment carrying boxes. A U-Haul van was parked on the street. I opened the door for the couple.

"Moving day, huh?" I grinned.

"Yep." They bobbed their heads and smiled. I had an idea.

"Would you mind if I looked at your apartment?" In older buildings like this, the apartments were all different, and it was fun to see the diverse layouts.

"Go for it," the fellow said. "The door is open. We're done."

"Thanks." Fido went ahead of me into the vacant apartment, drawn inside by new smells. A narrow kitchen with tall, white-painted cabinetry was to the left, a living room was walled off from the kitchen, the bath and bedroom were at the far end. The place was a decent size. Mentally, I calculated, if the top half of the wall that divided the kitchen from the living room was removed, it would open up the kitchen and be more aesthetically pleasing.

"Great place, huh?" Joel had stepped in while I was re-imagining the space. He was minus the cat, and despite our clash about a tenant's complaint, he looked handsome and charming. I cursed myself for thinking such thoughts.

Still irritated from the written warning he had given, I sputtered, "Tom Kat set Fido off barking. He was on the fire escape again, peeping."

"That so?"

"Yes. He. Was," I snapped. I hoisted Fido to my shoulder and stared at the laid-back maintenance man. His eyes held a glint of laughter, and his mouth stifled a grin.

"I'll tell that to the owners."

"Who complained?" I was still hot under the collar but had simmered down. Fido licked my cheek while I held him.

"They don't tell me who. They just tell me that someone called and complained." He shrugged. "I'll try to keep a tighter rein on Tom Kat." He tilted his head, his chin lowered, and his shoulders relaxed.

"Do that." I felt my face flush. My fair complexion could go from a pale pallor to crimson with little provocation. It was likely the color of a tomato.

"Are you interested in this apartment?" he asked, looking around. "You have done a great job making yours a home. It would be a shame to move."

"I don't want to move unless I have to," I said, glaring, holding his gaze a moment longer than needed. "I like the character of these older buildings. It is fun to see what the other apartments look like." Gesturing toward the unit, I asked, "Have you ever considered removing part of the wall between the kitchen and living room? It would make it more modern but maintain the charm of the apartment."

He studied the wall separating the kitchen and living room.

"I see what you mean. That would open the kitchen to the living area. But," he countered, "the renter would lose cupboards."

"They would still have the upper cabinets for storage across the back wall and the bottom cupboards by the sink." I reflected on the layout. "It's a one bedroom, so how much stuff could someone have?"

"You would be surprised. Many residents live here for several years." He grinned. "We try to accommodate people." At my raised eyebrows, he added, "We really do."

The young man who was moving returned. "Here are the keys and my new address. Thanks, Joel. It's been a pleasure."

"I'll request the damage deposit today. The place looks fine." Joel and the tenant shook hands, and the fellow left.

"You have great ideas, Merry. I will pass that on to the owners for future occupants. The place is rented now. I'll clean and paint this weekend for the new tenants who move in on Monday."

***

After a brisk walk with Fido, we headed to the store. Aunt Liz would come the next day. Although she would bring lunch, I was woefully low on groceries, and I needed dog chow. With my list in hand, we trekked to my aging sedan. I opened the back door and let Fido jump in. With cooler weather, it was the best time of the year for car rides. Fido waited in the car while I shopped. After loading the provisions, I gave him a treat from the stash I kept in the glove box for his patience.

At home, while unloading the groceries, the phone rang. I grabbed the phone as I stashed the canned tuna and soups.

"Guess who I saw tonight?" Kris exclaimed. Her voice held laughter, demanding.

"Who?" I paused and closed the cupboard.

"Mr. Pink Cadillac!"

"Randy?"

"The same." She paused, breathless. "He was with another woman. A tall, leggy blonde. He was putting a suitcase in his car. It looked like it was hers."

"Where were you?"

"At the strip mall."

"He must have had another coupon." I laughed. *He said he would be out of town for work.*

"So, you aren't upset?" she asked.

"No. Why would I be?"

"He is tall and handsome in a goofy way. He's employed and eligible. Okay, he has some issues." She giggled.

"We didn't connect." I sighed, exasperated.

"If you say so."

"I say so. No way."

"Let's look at those dating sites this weekend," she suggested.

"I can't. My resume and the Reindeer Festival mission calls."

"Oh, yeah," she said drolly. "Benjamin's homework."

"Maybe we can keep our jobs if he likes our ideas," I offered.

"Harrumph. Benjamin looks like a scrooge to me."

"Yeah. A scrooge who owns our jobs," I said, resigned.

"Harrumph," she repeated.

"I totally agree," and closed the cupboard door. "But right now, he's our only option."

Joel

Merry's ideas are awesome for updating the apartments. The buildings had charm, but keeping the charm and modernizing them would be the best of both worlds. If word got out that Holly Street and Ivy Lane were updated, and hip, I would have no problem keeping them fully occupied. The rumblings of the sharks of real estate moving into Reindeer Falls and luring tenants away were getting louder. The couple that moved had purchased a house. So, that was great for them. I rented the unit the day they gave notice, but news of big buyers nagged at me. The days of quick rentals could change.

I felt a rush watching her move through the apartment and coming up with a new design. The passion she had for design was exciting, and I wanted to be around her more. I hated giving that second warning, but I had no choice. The mutt was disturbing the peace. I would keep a closer tab on Tom Kat. Cats and dogs are challenging. Just like Merry Ernst. She intrigues me.

Chapter 12

Merry

The next day, Aunt Liz knocked promptly at noon.

"Guess you're the best security a gal could have." Scooping up the barking dog, I let her in.

"I brought lunch from the deli," she announced, putting her bags on the kitchen table. "Hi, Fido. I brought you a treat too." She reached out to pet him, and he leaned against my shoulder, eyeing her hand. "Okay, you're not my friend without a treat."

"He's very protective," I offered.

"Yes. He is. Good dog," she agreed. We laughed, and he sniffed her hand and gobbled the morsel.

She settled in the living room while I served mugs of steaming hot coffee. I sat next to her and took out a notepad, and she slipped on her readers.

"The Reindeer Falls Festival is the biggest event in town, so a decorating competition for the apartment buildings might be fun," I said. "The residents could decorate their unit doors, and then the owners could go all out on the main entries, with garland, lights, and wreaths.

Each building could have a theme, Santa and Elves, and Rudolph, the red-nosed reindeer, of course. There must be reindeer!" I chuckled. "Crafts for the children, and maybe a pet costume competition."

"For dogs?" she asked.

"Both cats and dogs, although it might be tough to get Tom Kat in a costume." I laughed. Then, soberly, I added, "The building super gave me another written warning."

"He didn't!" She took off her glasses and studied me. "I don't like the sound of that."

"It wasn't Fido's fault," I protested. "Tom Kat was lounging on the fire escape outside the kitchen window, peeping again."

"Do you know who complained?"

"No idea. Joel said it's confidential between the owners and the renter who has the beef."

"So, that's two now." She mulled over the news, her brows furrowed.

"Yes." I frowned, sipping my coffee. "Three written warnings and we're out."

"Don't worry. They will not evict you and Fido!" she said, and added, "If they do, you can stay with me!"

"That is awesome, Aunt Liz! Hope it doesn't come to that. I have to stand on my own two feet and fend for my pet." Setting my cup on the table, I pulled Fido into my lap.

"Don't be silly. It's what family does."

I studied Aunt Liz. "Thanks. I appreciate it." Clearing my throat, I asked tentatively, not wanting to stir up bad memories, "Why didn't you and my mother get along?" I had heard snippets of a feud between the sisters but had few memories of them, before my parents died in the car accident. Aunt Liz was the mother I knew. With no children of her own and a young widow herself, it was just a shadow recall of an earlier time.

"We took different directions," she said, musing aloud. "Your mother married young, had you, and I wanted a career. It wasn't so much that we didn't get along. We approached life differently, and that led to disappointment that perhaps the road each of us took was lacking. No one's life is perfect."

"She was unhappy?"

"Each of us had our disappointments." Her mouth puckered. "I tried to make life better for you, to honor your parents. So, we need to find you a husband! A good husband!" Throwing back her long tresses, her round cheeks flushed, and she tittered.

"Oh boy. I had a husband. Derrick," I reminded her.

"A *better* husband," she said firmly, arching her brows. "Someone with the potential to be a good father."

"Yes, Aunt Liz." When Aunt Liz lifted her brows, I had best not challenge her. She fixed her blue eyes on me. Avoiding her stare, I asked. "More coffee?" She nodded, and I leaped to refill the coffee mugs.

"Are you ready to eat?" I asked.

"Yes." She rose and followed me into the kitchen.

"These look wonderful!" I unloaded the deli bag containing chicken Caesar wraps. "Dessert too! My favorite, brownies!" My mouth watered, and I put out dishes for each of us.

"Yes. And everything is calorie free!" She laughed.

"Of course it is." I nodded and chuckled.

Fido whined and sniffed the aromas. I took out milk bones for him, and we sat at the table. I slipped him doggie tidbits while we inhaled our food.

"Should we have dessert in the living room?" I asked.

"Yes, let's," she agreed, and we headed back to the living room. After we savored the fudgy brownies, we sat back on the sofa and patted our stomachs. "I have another prospect for you." She had recovered from our food fest. I groaned. "Oh hush. I think he has potential. More than Randy."

"Who?" I asked. "I think Randy is content with his life as it is."

"Yes. He may be set in his ways, not as willing to share as you need to be in a committed relationship."

"The coupon thing?" I asked.

"Yes! When I thought it through, if he was helping a family member, a few words of explanation would help. Saving money is fine. But a new relationship is different."

"It made me feel icky," I admitted. "Too early. Even Dutch treat would have been better." Shrugging, I wrinkled my nose.

"Anyway, I have a new prospect for you." She sounded triumphant.

"Okay." I was cautious.

"He's a student in my yoga class." She beamed. "Very handsome, wonderful balance."

"Uh, huh? What do you know about him?"

"Not a lot. But if he is as genuine as he appears in his yoga practice, he would be a splendid match."

"So, you haven't talked to him much?" My nose itched, and I rubbed it.

"Well, no." She appeared wounded.

"What's his name?"

"I don't know yet. But he says namaste in the most sensual manner," she said, her eyelashes fluttering.

"Aunt Liz!"

"What? We are trying to get husband and father material in a package for you." She fluffed her hair.

"Any more festival ideas? Benjamin wants them by the end of the month."

"Hmm." She peered at me. "Benjamin wants a lot of lists these days." I had told her about listing our duties and the time to perform them.

"Tell me about it." I gave an eye roll and sipped coffee.

"How many buildings does TREM manage in the town?"

"Right now, three."

"So, Rudolf, Santa and the Elves. Maybe Snoopy?"

"Snoopy would be perfect with a pet costume contest, with Charlie Brown judging," she exclaimed. "Fido could wear a costume, too!"

"He could." I smiled at him snuggled next to me on the sofa. "How about a Gingerbread House theme?"

"Ooh, with Christmas cookies. There is Kwanzaa and Hanukkah, of course; you want to appeal to a broad population, so a nondenominational bent with popular characters," she said.

"That should be enough. Benjamin and TREM can pick from my list and Kris's." Satisfied, I jotted down the festivities that we had brainstormed. Hopefully, it would transform TREM's buildings into one of Reindeer's fabulous events.

We gave each other a high five and hugged. And she left, both of us satisfied with our festival ideas.

Chapter 13

Merry

"Randy!" I was surprised to see his name on the phone display Sunday morning.

"I hope you don't mind my calling on short notice?" he asked.

"No. That's okay." In the back of my mind, I would level with Randy and tell him I only wanted to see him as a friend.

"Would you and Fido want to join me for a walk this morning? We could do lunch or brunch?"

I thought quickly; a walk would be an easy way to introduce the topic. Over the phone seemed cold.

"Yes, let's go for a walk. But I have plans for later." I crossed my fingers.

"About 10 o'clock, in an hour?"

"That would be great."

Randy rapped at my door at the agreed upon time, and I hurried out, dressed in sweats and a hoodie with Fido leashed, excited to walk. I locked the door and faced him.

"You're in a hurry?" he asked.

"Sort of. I have plans."

"Sure." He smiled broadly and ran a hand through his thin hair.

We headed down the staircase and outside. I winced when I saw his Caddy parked on the street in front of the building. It was hard to miss.

We chatted a few minutes about the weather and how it had been a glorious Indian summer, lamenting the inevitable change to heavy winter coats and boots. I sneaked a look at him. He was athletic and jovial. A man used to everything coming together for him. I recalled Kris' mention of him out with a tall blonde. It fit.

On the path that ran alongside the riverwalk, I gathered my courage.

"So, how was your business trip?" I asked.

"What? Oh, that." He appeared startled and gave a short laugh. "It was fine. The company is reorganizing. They want to change the lead on the project."

"Oh?"

"They don't think the woman in charge is doing the job." He shrugged.

"Uh, huh? So, did the company business take the full week?" I glanced over at him while we picked up our pace. There was silence while we trekked.

"Uh, no. Why do you ask?" He stumbled on an uneven portion of the path, frowned, and regained his footing.

Against my better judgment, knowing that it was too early to question, and that I had decided friendship was best for us, I blurted. "A friend of mine saw you out."

"Out? Where?"

"She said you were with a tall blonde woman," I said delicately. "Near the strip mall."

"Oh." He flushed. "Yes. She is a friend. She's staying at my house until she gets an apartment."

"Uh, huh."

He frowned. "I am concerned about your questions. There seems to be a level of emotional attachment that's too early."

"Uh, huh." Any slack I would have given Randy was gone. If the woman was only a friend, it seems he would have said something when we went out. My trust had been crushed with Derrick. Too soon or not, I wanted the truth up front. Checking my watch, I said, "Oh my. I must go. Thanks for the walk. We'll take it from here."

My apartment was in view. I took off at a light trot. Randy lingered behind and slowed to a walk. A few paces from his car, I turned and waved. He had stopped to watch, perplexed, with his hands resting on his hips.

Entering the building, we nearly smacked into Joel and Tom Kat. Fido spied the cat and yipped.

"It's just the cat," I said. To avoid any altercations, I scooped him up and greeted them. "Hi."

"So that's who belongs to the pink Cadillac?" Joel drew out a chuckle, watching through the glass entry door as Randy got behind the wheel.

"Yes." I flushed. "It was his mother's car."

"He couldn't afford to buy his own car?" His eyes crinkled at the corners with laughter.

I snickered and sidestepped the question. "It'd be an awesome car in the Halloween parade."

"Yeah. That is coming soon, too. This town sure likes its festivals." He chuckled.

I had been so preoccupied with thoughts for the festivities that Halloween, another Reindeer favorite, would be upon us within ten days.

***

After lunch on Friday, Benjamin stood by his door and waved me into his office. He had called Kris in before lunch and she had left while I was on break. It had been too busy that morning to ask if she had any other inspirations. Vainly, looking for her, I grabbed my paper and headed to his office.

Benjamin sat, leaning back in his chair, while I perched on the edge of mine. I offered the list of ideas I had printed out the night earlier. He viewed the page, nodding.

"Looks good, Merry. You understand this is a work product and belongs to TREM." He threw the sheet on the desk and sat up. He cleared his throat, steepled his hands, and peered through thick-rimmed glasses, and said, "TREM has decided to go in another direction."

"What do you mean?" I waited for what seemed an eternity.

"We won't be needing your help at the new office." My stomach dipped, and I felt my face flame red. He reached into his top drawer and brought out a check and a letter of termination, adding, "This is two weeks of severance pay. You may clear your desk and leave now."

"But, but," I sputtered.

"Thank you for your service, Merry." He stood. I left; my head held high, angry that he had duped me. Kris had been right. The company had kept us on to ensure they had a smooth transition and to take our suggestions for the town's festival.

In a funk, I loaded my coffee mug and Fido's picture into my handbag. Benjamin stood in the doorway of his office, with arms crossed, watching. I glanced over at Kris' station and saw that her desk was uncharacteristically neat; her red mug was gone. She must have gotten the news that morning. I gritted my teeth, grabbed my coat, and left.

Ugly tears came as I slunk home, my collar up around my neck, avoiding eye contact with the other walkers. Fido went into delirious fits of barking when I burst through the door, a full three hours earlier than normal. I scooped him up and held him close while he licked my face. He quieted, giving me anxious looks while more tears came.

My phone rang, and I checked the Caller ID. It was Kris. Dabbing my cheeks with a tissue, I answered.

"You were right. TREM was going to fire us all along."

"Yes. But not before they took our festival ideas," she said.

"Bastards!" I snapped.

"What will you do?" she asked. "I've put out feelers."

"Get another job. What else can I do?" I took another tissue and wiped my eyes. "Do you have any leads?"

"Maybe." There was silence while she thought. I could almost hear the gears turn. "They can't keep our ideas."

"Sure, they can," I said.

"Did you put in for pay for the time you spent outside of work?" she asked.

"No."

"There is no way they can claim ownership of our ideas. It is a free world!" she declared.

"They asked us for our ideas. It was for work. We wrote them down and gave them the suggestions," I reminded her.

"Let them sue." She sneered.

I hesitated, then giggled. Her defiant tone sent me into more mirth. She joined me in sputtering laughter. After settling down, I said, "There's nothing that unique about decorating the buildings with a theme. I am going to ask Joel if I can decorate the building entries with different motifs."

"Why?"

"Just to prove to TREM that they can't rip off their employees. We are talking about people's lives," I said, echoing her anger.

"Do you think he'd go for it?"

"Why not? It would be excellent PR for the owners."

"Do you like Joel?" Her voice was bubbly and teasing.

"No!" I was aghast. "He's got a cat with an attitude."

"Cat Attitude?" Her voice trembled with mirth. She gasped between fits. "How many buildings does he manage?"

"Two. This one and another on the opposite side of the river. If you take the walkway over the bridge, it's on the edge of downtown. They only allow cats there. No dogs."

"Hmm. Sounds like canine discrimination."

"No dogs. I guess so." I laughed and stroked Fido, who looked up at me, uncertain. He seemed to understand my side of the conversation.

"I need to call Aunt Liz and tell her about TREM."

"Maybe she'll have a lead on gainful employment," Kris said soberly. "It's a crummy time of year to fire people!"

"They gave you severance pay?" I asked.

"A little. You?"

"Two weeks."

"They gave me two weeks for every year I worked," she sputtered. "Cheapskates."

"It's something." I sniffed. I was already thinking of decorating themes for Joel.

"It won't last long. I had better get moving," she said. "We'll talk more later."

I called Aunt Liz. She cheered me up with a promise to shake any branches with her network of yoga and knitting friends. She had retired from nursing early and knew the medical field was not my jam. My stomach churned, and I felt faint when I saw blood. A fact she'd noted whenever I got shots, and the nurse finally found a vein.

I fed Fido and dined on a gooey grilled cheese, to heck with dairy and carbs. It was comfort food all the way. After dinner, we went out for our walk. The fresh air and wind soothed my nerves as I strolled beside river, and my spirits lifted, seeing the cheerful decorations on streetlights along the pathway.

Joel greeted me on the steps to the building. "Great night for a stroll." He wore his tan work jacket and faded blue jeans.

"It is." I nodded. "Where's Tom Kat?"

"I left him inside while I worked on the washers and dryers. Got new machines." He grinned.

"That's great." The old washing machines in the basement that serviced the building were out of commission often.

I grimaced. The weight of the day's events hit, and I wiped my nose, and he looked at me curiously. "Is anything wrong?"

"TREM let me, and a coworker go today." I blushed furiously. Angry and embarrassed, I was not ready to say fired.

"That's rough." He was sympathetic. "Right before the holidays." He added, "TREM has a reputation for being lean and mean."

"You've heard of them?"

"Yep. Most of the building owners and maintenance managers know TREM and how they operate. They don't take care of their buildings and raise the rents so high that tenants move in and out a lot. The owners here have fended off their offers a few times."

"Oh, my." My stomach dipped at the idea TREM had tried to buy the building I lived in. "One of my final job duties was to generate ideas for the town's festival to build goodwill, so there would be less resistance when they wanted to buy more buildings. Would the owners here be interested in a festival decorating competition?"

"That sounds like a hoot! Give TREM a run for their money," Joel said. "Would you, do it?"

"I'd love to!" The possibility excited me.

"If you come up with the plan, I will buy the stuff and hang the decorations. If we win, we'll split the cash prize 50/50."

"That works for me. You don't have to run it past the Goldmans?"

"No," He grinned. "They pretty much let me do what I want."

"That's a nice work situation."

"Can't beat it." He chuckled. I felt a twinge of envy at his confidence. Micro-managing was typically a part of every job. It had to be a relief to be trusted by your employer.

"How about I put together some design ideas, and we'll go over them?" I asked, feeling a rush of inspiration.

"We'll have to work fast, though. Today is November first." He winked. "Reindeer loves its festivities."

"How about stopping over on Sunday? It will give me time to plan. Sunday afternoon after lunch, say 1:00?" Joel's interest in my design ideas sparked my happy place, and I relaxed, my defenses wavering. Maybe he wasn't all bad.

"Sounds good." He nodded.

"You got my rent check, too?" I had slipped the check in the payment box before work that morning. I was relieved that I had done it before getting the heave-ho.

"Yes, ma'am. Right on time," he drawled.

"See you Sunday then." Buoyed by his enthusiasm and the prospect of a creative project, I bounded up the stairs to my apartment with Fido leading the way. "Maybe we're off the hook," I whispered.

I grabbed my laptop and started scrolling for festival ideas that could spur my imagination into a winning idea for the Goldmans. After two hours of googling with my notebook and copying and pasting inspiration photos, I put the computer away, satisfied with my progress.

Chapter 14

Merry

Early Saturday morning, Aunt Liz called. "Would you have time for a quick bite today?"

"I always have time for food."

We met at the front counter of our favorite deli. Aunt Liz enveloped me in a huge hug, squeezing my shoulders.

"Do not worry about the job, Merry. If it was meant to be, it will be." I loved Aunt Liz. But sometimes she could be a little too cheery. I never quite knew what that saying was about. If it was, it was. I needed a job.

"Let's order," she urged. Against my protestations, she insisted on paying, and we grabbed our food trays, poured hot steaming coffee from the pot at the kiosk, and found a coveted booth where we could sit and visit.

"I have just the thing to get your mind off your troubles." She smiled mischievously.

"A new job?" I asked, hopefully.

"Better," she said. I frowned. "We will work on the job. Remember the fellow I told you about in my yoga class?"

"Oh, oh." I gulped.

"Do not poo poo. His name is Stephan. He's a hairdresser for that fancy place where all the news people get their hair done for television."

"I can always use help in the hair department." I grinned. My long locks fell flat today, and they suffered from a lack of brushing. I wore faded jeans, had thrown a jean jacket over a sweater, and dashed out, smelling the crisp air, thinking snow could rule soon.

"Don't we all?" she asked. "Anyway, he has the most beautiful long mane. Sometimes he wears his hair back in a ponytail or in one of those man buns. So cute." Her eyes twinkled, and her dimples deepened.

"Uh, huh."

"He's hip, too," she gushed. "He has a pierced ear and wears a diamond stud. Very classy. Not too much, just enough."

I popped a morsel of quiche into my mouth and thought.

"So, a diamond stud? Which ear?" I held her gaze.

"Which ear? Let me see, the right one, I believe." She slapped the side of her head, her eyes widened. "You don't think?"

My brows rose, and I said, "Right, is wrong. Wrong for me."

"Oh, dear. He is so handsome, too." She inhaled and lifted her shoulders.

"I'm sure he is." I tore off a piece of Danish. "First things first, I need to find gainful employment."

"I put out a couple of feelers and will float you a loan." She was cheerful.

I winced, hating to be in debt to anyone, even Aunt Liz. "I'm okay for now." It was a white lie. The severance pay, along with my little savings, would be depleted soon. "The good news is"—I cleared my throat — "until such a time of gainful employment, there's no need for a dog sitter on Thursdays." Shrugging, I said, "I'll be home, and class will wrap up soon, anyway."

"Fido and I have the best times on Thursdays!" She looked disappointed.

"There will be other opportunities. Winter is coming. It won't be as easy to get out and walk. We'll visit indoors."

"Hmm. I suppose you're right. But I am first on the list for dog sitting."

"Deal!"

"What happened with Randy?" she asked wistfully, tilting her head. "He seemed like a great catch."

"The last word from Randy was that I was too serious, too soon." I studied my coffee, avoiding her steady gaze.

"Really?" She was dumbstruck.

"Kris told me she saw him with another woman. There was a suitcase involved. He claimed she was a friend, but he was touchy about the whole thing."

"Protested a little too much?"

"Yes."

"Pity." She sniffed. "You said his place was a disaster."

"That would be flattery." I giggled. She caught my giggles and snorted, gasping, "Hit the road, Jack, er, Randy." And snickered. "There's a song, you know."

"Good riddance." I chuckled, then looked at my watch. "Time to go. I have to firm up a game plan for the festival."

"You're still doing the festival? How does that work, now that your job is done?"

"Joel, the building maintenance man, wants to compete for the prize money. He said if I came up with the grand plan, he would purchase and hang the decorations. He is coming over tomorrow, and we're going over the designs."

"Oh, my." She laughed. "He is so cute with that black cat on his shoulder. You're sure Fido won't mind your spending time with a feline and his owner?"

"Tom Kat won't be there. At least, I doubt he would bring his cat." I shrugged into my jacket.

"Oh, but his scent will be," she quipped, grabbing her handbag. "But then, opposites attract." She winked, draping a turquoise scarf around her coat collar. Her eye color popped with the scarf's hues. "Hug," she demanded as we lingered at the table.

We parted ways outside the deli, and I thanked the gods for Aunt Liz. She had brightened my day.

Joel

I was pumped about spending time with Merry, going over plans for a run at the Reindeer Festival prize money. Judging from her apartment, she had talent. Her devotion to the mutt was inconvenient. But she had depth, a trait Patricia had lacked. Merry had me hooked, and I wanted to spend more time getting to know every part of her life.

From her hang dog expression, I could tell she'd had a tough day. What a dickwad her boss must have been. Companies that lay off people before the holidays were nasty. She was perfect in every way. A little short. Okay, petite. Long brownish hair with a hint of blonde, luminous eyes that made my stomach melt.

And that pink Cadillac. That's a joke. What guy drives a pink car? What's his deal, anyway? Merry said it had been his mother's car. How do you spell cheap? She deserves better than a bald guy driving his mother's cast-off car.

Sunday afternoon can't come soon enough. But the little mutt is a problem. That dog wants his mistress to himself. Maybe treats will work.

Chapter 15

Merry

After meeting Aunt Liz, I stopped for the mail on the way to my apartment, sorting through the bills and flyers as I strolled. From a distance, I spotted a small, dark object at the base of my door and hesitated, hearing Fido's loud sniffs from inside.

"Gaaah!" Dropping my mail, I unlocked the door and hustled inside. The dog continued sniffing, whining in protest as I blocked him. Hurriedly, I dialed maintenance. Joel answered on the third ring.

"Your cat left a dead mouse outside my door!"

He paused and asked in a droll tone, "Can you describe the mouse?"

"It isn't funny!" Dead objects made my knees go weak and my body squirm. "Could you please just take it away?" My adrenalin was high, and my voice rose to an even higher pitch.

"How do you know it was my cat?"

"I *don't* know. But he is the only cat I know in the building!"

"That doesn't make him the culprit." He teased.

"Please!"

He gave a low chuckle.

"Be right there. You should be flattered. Cats don't leave mice for just anyone—"

I hung up.

I was on high alert until Joel's footsteps sounded in the hallway. The noises outside my door suggested a rustle of a plastic baggie and paper.

"All clear now." He rapped and gave a low chuckle.

"Hold up the bag so I can see it." I peered through the security hole.

He stepped back, waved a brown paper bag, then picked up the scattered mail as I opened the door.

"For someone who lives alone, you sure are tense," he said, amused, studying me.

"I live with Fido." I scooped up the dog and held him on my shoulder. Leashed, he was ready to go out. With my free hand, I took the mail. "Thank you," I said stiffly.

"My pleasure." He grinned. "We're still on for tomorrow? You haven't changed your mind because of Tom Kat's tomfoolery? Not that there is anything that proves he's the culprit."

"Still not funny." I glared. "Yes. We are still on. One o'clock." Fido leaned toward Joel, sniffing the air by the bag.

"See you then. Bye." He winked and left me speechless, weak in the knees from the sight of the dead mouse, and the genial way air he had disposed the rodent.

***

When Joel arrived the next afternoon, I had prepared a rough drawing of the main entry for each building on a sketch pad. I ushered him to the tight living room, noting the room got smaller with his height and broad shoulders. He wore a blue-plaid flannel shirt and blue jeans. We sat on the sofa. The sketchpad, laptop, and copies of decorating ideas filled the coffee table.

"Coffee?" I asked. "Or I have water and cola. It's diet cola."

"Coffee is great. Black." He leaned over the table and studied the sketches.

I poured a mug of fresh java and placed it on the coffee table next to him, then sat down and cradled my cup, sipping the brew as I looked over his shoulder.

"This looks awesome!" he exclaimed. "Winter Wonderland. Seasonal, not too much glitter."

"Red berries could replace the Christmas bulbs, so it could stay up through the winter. It would be pretty to look at through a cold season."

"Excellent." He nodded. "What ideas did you pass on to the competition?"

"Rudolph and Santa. Santa's Elves."

"Your co-worker gave ideas, too?"

"She suggested Scrooge or Mr. Cratchit." I snickered.

"Yeah. That would be right up their alley." He snorted.

"That's what we thought," I said with a grimace.

"Let's go with it," he said. "Winter Wonderland will unify the two buildings, and the theme will carry through the season. I like it!"

He held his cup up to meet mine in a toast, and I blinked, feeling a spark as he met my gaze. Blushing, I glanced away and asked, "So, you'll get the supplies?"

"Yep. You have to help me shop." He stood up. Fido watched, alert to his every move.

"Now?"

"No time like the present. We can get most of the supplies at The Home Store." The store was on Main Street by the strip mall where Randy and I had had our coupon date. "Unless you have something else to do?"

"Perfect." I grabbed my coat, leashed Fido, and we were out the door. I felt a little thrill that Fido was included. While Joel headed to his work truck, I detoured to the elimination area. He opened both passenger doors to the dual cab pickup. After lifting the dog in the back, I sat in front, helpless to stop grinning. Gazing out the window, I composed myself, feeling the heat from Joel's body in the tight cab, and tugged my jacket closer.

We studied The Home Store's section devoted to Christmas and seasonal items. Absently, I stroked Fido in the cart as we considered the goods.

"You point, and I'll put it in the cart," Joel said.

"I think we'll need a bigger cart," I bantered.

"No problem." He snagged a low trailer wagon. He followed while I pushed the shopping basket.

"What do you think?" I pointed at the flocked garland. "Around the main entries?"

"Works for me." He loaded the garland. "A few of them." He put them on his trailer.

"And these bulbs?" I pointed. "Maybe red, gold, and purple?"

"Excellent." He loaded the packs in my cart alongside a curious Fido.

"How about lights for the bushes by the entry?"

"Awesome." We picked out lights.

"What do you think of a pair of large pots outside of the entrance? Loaded with birch logs and evergreen boughs? With the garland, the bushes lit, and the pots, it will add depth to the display."

"Love it! Which ones?" We picked out two containers that complemented the building's red brick exterior.

"You're easy to please." I laughed.

"I aim to satisfy." He tilted his head and grinned.

A Thanksgiving display caught my eye, and I asked, "How about pumpkins on the straw bales as a nod to the holiday?"

"Great idea. Can't forget Thanksgiving. Easy enough to remove before the main events." He added the bales and pumpkins to his cart.

"I think we've done enough damage to your bank account." I felt my cheeks burn.

"Agreed." He grinned.

We checked out, and I loaded Fido along with the bounty into his truck.

"Whew, that was quite a haul," he said, and he started the engine. "How about a snack before we hang all this stuff?" My stomach warmed with the "we" in his sentence.

"I could eat." I was ravenous. All this shopping made me hungry.

"Burger Town?" he asked.

"Yes, let's go." The fast-food burger joint was a short five-minute drive on the way back to the buildings. "Fido can stay here for a few minutes while we eat," I said. "He has a fur coat."

"I'll let the truck run with the heat on." He nodded. "I have a spare key for just such times."

"Better!" I nodded happily.

He parked, and inside at the counter, I searched my purse for cash.

"Your money doesn't work here," he said with a grin.

"I can pay my way," I protested.

"No." He put his hand on my arm, stopping me. "You're doing me a favor." He turned to the counter person. "I'll have a cheeseburger, fries, and a coke." He nodded to me.

"Cheeseburger and a diet coke, please," I said.

Finding a booth, we sat and gazed out of the window. We watched Fido sit up, focused on the foot traffic, and we surveyed the haul in the bed of Joel's pickup.

"We did good." He smiled and bit into his burger.

"We did." My thoughts wondered about a man who liked to shop and decorate. Aunt Liz would be amazed. While we munched on burgers, I asked. "So, you have a girlfriend?" I blushed as I nibbled, avoiding eye contact.

"Nope." He dipped a French fry into catsup and stopped. "I did. Came close to getting married. Patricia left me when I quit the corporate world. She liked the suit, the job, and the perks of a megacorporation. It grew old for me. I changed, and I always wanted to work with my hands. So, now I maintain apartment buildings." He grinned. "And I love it. What's your story?" He leaned back, patting his stomach.

"Derrick, my ex-husband, found someone else."

"Sorry. It's his loss," he said.

"He waited until after I supported us through his program at the university, and it was my turn to go to school. His turn to pay the bills."

"Harsh."

"It was. I had no clue he wasn't happy."

"You were busy."

"Yes." I gulped. "So, was it serious between you and Patricia?"

"We were engaged."

I nodded. "That's serious."

"Had a big wedding planned, reception, the whole deal. She came from a big family. Me, not so much. She broke it off a week before the big day."

"OMG."

"Yep. At least we weren't standing at the altar." He shrugged. "It was for the best. Last I heard, she was going to marry a bigwig at the corporation. I am happy for her." He smiled gamely. "So, you aren't seeing Mr. Pink Cadillac?" His eyes were sparkling, teasing.

I choked. "God, no!" Tears threatened as I recovered from my coughing fit.

"Okay, then. Enough of this pity party. Let's get these decorations done." His smile warmed me as we collected our trash and headed out.

Outside, the air was lighter, the wind had subsided, and the sun had broken through clouds that had threatened rain most of the day. We got into his truck, and he drove to his parking spot in the back lot. Tom Kat lounged in the sunniest part of the space. His tail swishing, he leaped out of the way of the truck.

"Looks like someone is waiting for you," I said, glancing at Joel's profile. He beamed.

"Yeah! It does." He laughed. Fido sat up in the back, his paws against the rear of my seat. A low growl rumbled in his throat.

"Hush!" I stepped down from the truck and grabbed the dog. He wriggled and went into a full-on barking fit at Tom Kat. "Let me put him upstairs, then I'll help you unload," I muttered, dashing away.

"I'll be here." He bent down to stroke Tom Kat's head, and the cat leaped onto his shoulders as I left. I swear that cat smirked at us. I left Fido inside the apartment with a treat and a caution to settle down, and hustled back to the truck, where Joel had unloaded the outdoor pots and pumpkins. The cat wandered away while he worked.

"I'll start on the pot," I said. Joel placed the container, and I filled it with potting soil, placed the spruce tops, along with the other décor, then watered. While I worked on the arrangement, he hung the garland around the entry. Working in concert, we chatted and surveyed each other's progress as we decorated.

As a final touch, we added the hay bales and pumpkins to the display.

"It is getting late. Will we have enough light to do the other building entry?" I asked.

"Sure. Let's git 'er done. There will be enough light with the coach lights beside the entrance."

"Okay." I nodded. We loaded up the truck and headed over to Ivy Lane. It was dark when we finished the second display. We paused, viewing the results under dim light from the entrance and streetlights.

"Looks pretty dang good." Joel grinned.

"It does." I was happy with the effect. The flocked garland looked cheery, and the warm color of the pumpkins heralded the Thanksgiving holiday. "After Thanksgiving, I'll add the bulbs and holly sprays to fill in for Christmas."

"And I'll hang the lights." We gave each other a high five. "Fabulous job!"

"I should go. Tomorrow's Monday, and it's back to job hunting for me," I said.

"Let me drive you home."

"I'll walk. It's just a short stroll under the bridge, along the river to the building. The sidewalk is light enough with the streetlamps."

"Then I'll walk you home." He was matter-of-fact, picking up the spade and unused decorations.

"But you have the truck," I protested.

"I can walk back for the vehicle. Besides, I could stand to stretch my legs, too." He gazed at me, waiting.

"Okay. If you are sure?"

"Positive. A gentleman always walks a lady to her door." By the light of the entry, his smile was soft, and my heart took a leap.

"Nice!" It slipped out, and I blushed.

"I am. Nice." In companionable silence, we walked the few blocks to Holly Street. He left me at my door with a brief salute and the sound of Fido yipping. I went inside. Flustered, I locked the door and grinned.

"OMG, Fido. I might be in love." Joel had hit all the right buttons, taking Fido with us shopping, lunch, and then the walk home, with twinkling white lights wound around the poles lining the river frontage. How he could go from cad to a gentleman took my breath away.

Joel

I wasn't wild about bringing the dog to The Home Store, but what could I say? She had the ideas and the design skills. I had the muscle. Together, we would make it work. The mutt behaved himself; he didn't lunge at me outside of her place. I had to chuckle how he sniffed at the scent of the dead mouse.

I loved the way Merry worked. She had a vision that drove her to make the best displays. Her expression reflected the pleasure she had in designing, and the warmth she exuded was exhilarating. Even the shopping was tolerable. It was a buying expedition. She didn't dally, knew what she wanted, and that was exciting. She listened and seemed to 'get me.' I can't wait to see her again.

It was a relief to talk about Patricia and release the pain I felt by her bowing out of our engagement. The life change from corporate climber to a building super had been a fantastic opportunity to be my own boss, not subject to the whims of a corporation. Merry listened and didn't judge. Patricia wanted the three-piece suit and tie. She couldn't see or didn't want me. Merry understood, and that made her even hotter. Patricia's family were establishment with an ordered path. My path had been filled with potholes since losing my parents. I was grateful to the Goldmans for giving me this opportunity, but I didn't want to jinx it. I wasn't ready to tell Merry the Goldmans were my aunt and uncle.

That ex of hers had to have a serious screw loose to cheat on Merry. That's why she has her guard up. She thinks no one can burst her bubble of protection. She doesn't know Joel Connor.

Chapter 16

Merry

Early Monday morning, Kris called, "How's the job search going?"

"Not so good." I sat on my sofa, hunched over my computer on the coffee table, sifting through job listings on the state's website. My phone and a strong cup of coffee within reach.

"How about you?"

"I scored!" She giggled.

"Awesome! Tell me everything." I demanded.

"Remember, Mr. Bigg?"

"Yes. He only worked with Benjamin and didn't meet with staff, because he was too important."

"Well. I didn't tell you this, but one day when I was in the office, a man came in and sat down with Benjamin. While Benjamin walked him out, I snuck into his office and found a name, number, and address." She was gleeful. "I wasn't sure if he was the mysterious Mr. Bigg, but he was."

"I'm impressed." Kris had detective skills.

"I polished up my resume and paid him a visit." She paused, then blurted, "He hired me on the spot!"

"That's great! I'm happy for you. He's not with TREM, then?"

"No. He's a broker. He finds the buildings and handles the sales agreements for TREM. TREM manages the buildings, Benjamin does the mundane accounting and collects rent. He may want to add another agent. It could be you," she said.

"A sales agent? I'm not licensed."

"Easy peasy. You can learn. I'll keep you informed. Can I give him your name?"

"Of course. Please do. Thanks, Kris." I hung up. It was nice Kris remembered me, but sales agents worked on commission. I needed a steady income and went back to studying the job postings. While filling out an online application, the phone rang again.

"Busy day." I looked at the CID, and answered, "Aunt Liz, how are you?"

"Terrific! I have another potential mate for you," she trilled.

"Oh, boy." Joel and our last meeting flashed, and I winced, torn about saying anything.

"Now, Merry."

"Sorry. I didn't mean it that way, but I'm job hunting right now." Sighing, I knew she only wanted the best for me.

"That's okay. I won't keep you. But he's tall, dark, and handsome." Her voice trilled; she was pleased with the prospective mate.

"Okay." I sputtered. "So much for later."

"But how was your Sunday?"

"That's two buts," I countered.

"Uh, huh? How was it?" She persisted.

"It went well. We shopped for the decorations and then put them up. It was fun but a busy day."

"Oh! A man who shops *and* decorates."

Laughing, I said, "I knew you'd say that."

"And then?"

"What? He walked me home, and that's it." My voice drifted off, and I knew I sounded vague.

"Okay. Well, keep your options open. I'm giving tall, dark, and handsome your telephone number."

"I'm hanging up now." I clicked off. *There's nothing like Aunt Liz on a mission.*

I finished the application and hit send. Sitting back, I said, "Break time." Fido followed me to the kitchen and stood beside the counter, where the treat jar sat, waiting for a morsel. I slipped him a treat.

After taking a cookie for myself, I freshened my coffee and returned to my post in front of the computer. A quick rap at the door interrupted my browsing.

"Hey, Merry." It was Joel. His eyes twinkled, and his dimples deepened. My breath quickened seeing him.

"Hi." I folded my arms across my chest, quelling my reaction.

"Would you have time to check out this apartment? I'm painting for new tenants, and I could use a designer's touch with colors."

"Sure. I'll grab my keys." I locked up and headed up to the third floor. We entered No. 301. It was a large two-bedroom unit that faced the street. The floors were a well-worn hardwood, and the kitchen was a galley style, and like others, closed off from the living area.

"Open concept is all the rage right now," I commented.

"Yeah. Many of the buildings in this part of town were built when kitchens were separate and smaller," he said.

"So, no major renovations?"

"Not now. I want to rent it as soon as possible. Fresh paint is the limit." He flashed another dimpled smile and stood beside me. I felt the warmth of his closeness and flushed.

"How about sanding the floors?" I asked, keeping my voice neutral, trying to maintain a businesslike attitude.

He surveyed the room. "Yes. It needs it. I can refinish the floors."

"Shades of gray are big right now. I could help you paint."

"You're hired! I can pay you by the number of rooms in each apartment."

"Isn't that your job?" I asked. "Wouldn't the Goldmans object to paying someone else?"

"They're flexible. We have a few vacancies right now."

"Expunge the warnings for Fido, and it's a deal." I batted my lashes.

"You drive a hard bargain." He laughed. "I'll run it past the Goldmans. They make the rules."

At my raised eyebrows, he relented. "Okay, they're flexible. Deal."

"Why are people moving out?" I frowned.

"TREM is luring tenants away with two months free rent."

"That company again." I was grim. "What the average tenant doesn't know is that they will ratchet up the rent within the year to pay for those two 'free' months. Plus, they don't maintain. It looks like a great deal to start."

"Yep. That's the game." He shrugged and grimaced.

"Can I do this while I job hunt? Mostly nights, maybe some afternoons."

"No problem." He gave me a wide grin. "I'll get started on the floors today. We'll plan on painting Wednesday."

"You've got a deal." I held out my hand for a shake, and my faced flushed, warmed by his firm grasp and steady gaze. We shook on it.

"When I get the stain for the floors, I'll pick out color samples. Grays, right? Unless you can take a break and come with?"

"When?"

"In about ten minutes?"

"All right, then. I'll get my jacket." My heart did a little flip. "Meet you at your truck?"

"Excellent!"

For the second time in two days, we shopped The Home Store. I picked out colors for the apartment, and Joel bought supplies and rented a floor sander. After adding a bunch to his credit card, and loading the haul, we drove home. There, we trekked the items up to the vacant apartment.

"Thanks, Merry. I appreciate your help. The planters look great. The entries are awesome. I'm already getting more calls for the rentals."

"Curb appeal. I'll leave you to your work." Smiling, I headed back to my apartment and greeted Fido, who waited patiently. "Things are looking up," and I stroked him. Happy with the prospect of making money and using my design skills while looking for a full-time job. Buoyed that I could spend more time with Joel and pleased that Fido was off the eviction list.

I listened to a message on my answering machine.

"Hi, Merry. My name is Theodore. Your Aunt Liz gave me your number. I'd like to meet for coffee. You can reach me at...." I considered his tone. He did sound tall, dark, and handsome. His voice had a smooth, deep tenor, with a hint of sexy.

I jotted his name and number on a notepad. Coffee sounded safe. My mind drifted to Joel. He felt comfortable. His dimples were to die for, but I wasn't sure about him. Maybe he could be a friend while I searched for Mr. Right. Get used to being with the male species. Maybe Aunt Liz was right. It was time to leave Derrick in the past, move toward another, hopefully, better relationship. Theodore sounded interesting. I called him and set up a meeting over coffee the following Saturday. He was witty and self-assured, and I gave myself credit for getting out of my comfort zone. I didn't like to set up dates with strangers, but he was Aunt Liz approved.

***

That Wednesday, I filled out more applications and followed up on others. It was tedious work, and nothing seemed to click. Eager to stretch my legs and paint the apartment that Joel was working on, I headed up to check on the progress.

"The floors look great!" I said, as he waved me into the room.

"They do." He grinned. "You're dressed for work." He nodded approvingly. I wore a sweatshirt and grungy jeans, with my hair up in a ponytail. "You look great," he blurted. A bland look quickly covered his nervousness, and he asked, "Where do you want to start?"

"Smallest room first."

"Good choice. Bathroom." He carried a ladder to the area and spread the drop cloths.

"I'll tape off the room," I said.

"Go for it." We had settled on shades of gray for all the rooms. The bathroom and kitchen were the lightest, with a softer gray/blue for the bedrooms and living area. The kitchen cabinets were original, and we would freshen the white color. Joel would add new hardware, giving the kitchen a more contemporary feel. We chose new light fixtures to enhance the apartment. "I'll start on the kitchen cabinetry and light fixtures."

"Okay." I taped off the woodwork while he disappeared into the kitchen.

By the end of the day, we had the kitchen, bath, and one bedroom done, and were exhausted.

"How about dinner? My treat?" Joel asked. Construction dust covered his clothes, his hair was dotted with paint, and he looked beat.

"Thank you, but I'll call it a night and tuck in early." With a small smile, I brushed the hair from my face and wiped my forehead. Painting had been relaxing and given me time to think about my dilemma, and I wanted to follow up on my job search before I had a full-blown panic attack.

"So, I'll see you tomorrow morning?" I asked. "Unless I have an interview."

"Wouldn't miss it." He smiled. "Get some rest. It'll be another long day."

I headed to my place. I scarfed a sandwich while checking my email for messages from potential employers and found none. After dinner, I admired the newly decorated entrance as I passed the area with Fido. Then, I headed to the shower, tired. It had been a full day, and snippets of Joel's face and the work danced through my mind as I reviewed the day.

He'd been businesslike throughout the day, but attentive. It felt a little too cozy for a work situation. Whenever I glanced in his direction, he turned away. My gut melted, and I smiled when I caught him watching.

Did I find this man attractive, even with his attitude toward Fido? He hadn't included Fido on Monday, although he had invited him to come with us on our Sunday shopping trip. That was sweet. Monday was just a quick run.

Maybe he wasn't the cad he presented himself as. Maybe he was hurt more than he let on by Patricia ending their engagement. My shield was slipping, and my feelings were warming. I had to be wary.

Joel

Dang, I couldn't tempt her with dinner, but the time we spent working as a team to get the apartment ready had been exhilarating. She was cute, the way her face had scrunched up, concentrating on colors. She worked steadily and looked fabulous while she painted. It took everything I had to focus on the work in the apartment.

When she turned down dinner, the possibility there was someone besides the Cadillac man lurking crossed my mind. Was there someone she hadn't told me about? I knew we weren't dating. It would be off limits, or at least a conflict of interest, to date a tenant.

It is tempting to bend the rules. Besides, I make the rules, and I can break them.

Chapter 17

Merry

AFTER FEEDING FIDO THE next morning, we headed outside.

Shocked, I gasped and halted. Holding Fido back, I surveyed the scene. Someone had smashed the pumpkins against the sidewalk and the building. The innards and seeds oozed over the stoop and walk, making it slippery. They had scattered straw about. Vandals had ripped the spruce tips, birch logs, and other decor from the pots and strewn them over the lawn and entry.

"What the . .. !"

Joel joined me on the front stoop, carrying a black garbage bag.

"Oh, man!" He ran a hand through his hair and viewed the scene. "What a mess. The Goldmans called and said vandals had trashed the decorations."

"Why would anybody do that?" I wailed, exasperated. It felt personal, like someone was out to get me, us, the building.

"My guess is it's someone who doesn't want any competition for the Reindeer Festival."

"TREM?"

"Who else?" Disgust written on his face, as he bagged the remnants of the mess of gooey pumpkin innards, hay, and birch logs.

"I'll take Fido upstairs and get a broom." After settling the dog down, who reluctantly left the bounty of pumpkin remains, I returned.

Joel quickly gathered most of the litter, and I swept up the remains.

"What do you want to do about the decorations now?" Viewing his handsome face, I was afraid that he would quit the competition, and our work was for naught.

"I'll get more supplies, and we will redo. These people won't stop me." His expression was firm. Tying up the full garbage bag, he said, "I'll rig up a security camera. That will be a deterrent. I can monitor it with my cell phone."

"Okay." I nodded. "A camera should help. Should we call the police, make a report?"

"I will check the other building. If that one has been vandalized, then I'll call the cops and report it. The Goldmans hadn't been at the Ivy Lane building yet and hoped it was just this location. If so, it's probably kids in the neighborhood looking for a cheap thrill." He saw my expression, and added, "Little thugs."

Great, maybe they just hit the building I lived in.

"Are you okay to paint while I head over to Ivy Lane, and then to The Home Store?"

"Yes. I can do that." My job search hadn't produced any follow-up calls, and painting gave me time to think. And Joel was paying me.

"Good. I will let you in."

I finished painting the second bedroom about noon and was famished. Ready to start in the living room, I left Joel a note, "taking a lunch break" and went home.

Joel returned to the apartment where I had resumed painting at one o'clock. The work in the living room was moving quickly, and estimated my work would be done about 3:30 that afternoon.

"How did it go at Ivy Lane?" I asked.

"They left the building alone." He shrugged. "I bought a security camera for the front of this apartment, more pumpkins, and bales, and salvaged anything I could from the downstairs pots. They will need your touch to refurbish." He smiled.

"Okay. I can do that after I finish up here." Brushing stray hair from my face, I added, "You're sure we shouldn't report it? Someone else may have been vandalized."

"I'll call, but there wasn't any damage to the building. And we cleaned it up right away. It was a reflex action."

"Yeah. Maybe whoever did the damage is done." My nose twitched, uncertain.

He gazed at the living room and checked the bedroom. "Great job. I will go set up the camera." He nodded and left.

By the time I finished painting, cleaned the brushes, and headed downstairs to redo the pots, Joel was testing the camera with his phone. He had hosed the area down, set up the bales, and put out new pumpkins. After I redid the pots, we stood back and viewed the results.

"Looks good," I said, wiping my hands on my jeans.

"Like new," he agreed. "The camera's working, and I'll hang the fresh garland to camouflage it with the greenery."

"You should put out a sign that says, 'Smile—you are on camera.' Might make them think twice about damaging property," I countered. The vandalism still rankled.

"I hear you. It wouldn't look very inviting for the festival's competition, though." He grinned. "The fellow I bought the camera from told me to put out a sign and forget the camera."

"Really?" I was baffled. "Yeah." He laughed. "He said this was a safe area. The police have better things to do."

"Let's see how it goes. I will check on Fido and call it a day. Aunt Liz is stopping by after dinner."

"Thanks, Merry. I'll bring your check by on Saturday."

"Great. You're welcome. I'll be home in the morning." I nodded. Saturday's meeting with Aunt Liz's latest match was on for the afternoon. Tomorrow was Friday, and I hoped it would be a better day than today. I was beat, and

Aunt Liz promised to stop by and tell me all about Mr. Tall, Dark, and Handsome. The sound of his voice was enticing, and my stomach had done a brief flutter during our telephone conversation.

***

"Well, you've been busy!" Aunt Liz commented after my tirade about the damage to the decorations and painting the upstairs apartment.

"You have, too." We sat in the living room, and I frowned, focused on the glass of white wine I had poured for each of us. "What can you tell me about Theodore?"

"He called?"

"Yes. He sounds divine," I admitted.

"He is Julia's godson. You remember Julia from the knitters?"

"Can't say that I do." My forehead creased, recalling the group.

"Well, maybe you don't know her. She is a new member and thought her godson would be a good match for you. So, why not? At least it isn't that online matching stuff. You can check him out."

Aunt Liz's disdain for online dating reminded me of the profile Kris had started for me. I made a mental note to see how the site looked.

"We set up a coffee meeting for Saturday." I couldn't say 'date.' The word scared me.

"Sounds perfectly fine. He is a lawyer."

"Maybe that's why he goes by Theodore? It seems formal." Frowning, I sipped my wine.

"Ask him tomorrow. I am excited for you!" she exclaimed. "This will get you out there."

"Aunt Liz." I cleared my throat. "I hope I am not a major topic of conversation in your club. It would be embarrassing." I flushed.

"Oh, heavens. No worries. We talk about all kinds of people." She smiled; her lashes fluttered.

Wincing, I asked, "What kind of projects have you done lately?"

"Knit, schnit. There is a lot going on with the group right now. We will get back to it. Don't you fret." She patted my knee, and I groaned.

"I'll let you get your beauty rest, not that you need it, dearie, but I want you to look fresh for Theodore tomorrow."

"We'll walk you to your car." I leashed Fido one last time and followed Aunt Liz to her SUV. About to drive away, she rolled down her window and admonished, "Call me!"

She left, and while I pondered tomorrow's meeting with Theodore, I surveyed the outdoor décor. Satisfied it was intact, I waved at the camera and headed upstairs.

Chapter 18

Merry

A KNOCK AT MY door early Saturday morning disturbed my slumber. I threw on a robe and checked the peephole. It was Joel. Fido barked behind me, furious at the intrusion.

"What's up?" I wiped the sleep from my eyes and cracked the door open with the chain in place.

"The vandals hit the Ivy Lane building decorations overnight." He was grim-faced, and frustration seeped from his shoulders.

"No!"

"Can you help me put the display back together?" he asked.

"Of course. But I have plans for early afternoon and must be back by noon." It would be tight, returning to my apartment, sprucing up, and meeting Theodore. "Sooner would be better than later."

"No problem. I'll buy breakfast on the way, and we will do what we did yesterday." He muttered, "Hooligans. I'll take pictures of the damage and call the cops this time."

"Good idea. Is this building, okay?"

"Yep. They must have known not to mess with it. By the way, you were on camera last night." He winked. My face reddened, and I squirmed. I recalled my casual wave to the camera, not thinking that Joel could be watching. At least I had been dressed, not like now, wearing my purple robe.

"So, it works. That is good." Satisfied, I added, "I'll get ready, feed Fido, and meet you at the truck."

"Bring Fido. It will be good for him to get out," he urged.

My heart melted. "He'd love that."

Joel stopped at a fast-food place, and we ate breakfast sandwiches and sipped hot coffee on our way to the building.

I groaned when I saw the entry to the second building. It was like the movie *Groundhog Day*. Vandals had smashed pumpkins and littered the walk, along with straw and decorations from the containers.

"Yep. They did a number on it," Joel said. "At least they didn't set fire to the straw." He scowled. "We'll get it cleaned up and salvage what we can, to redo the pots.

"Who on earth would do this?" I demanded.

"Don't know." Joel was grim. "Someone who has a lot of time on their hands or wants to enter the festival with no competition. I called the cops to make a report. They should be here soon." Joel took pictures, and we waited on the stoop until a squad car drove up. He talked to the young community service officer, who took notes, while Joel explained what had happened at the Holly Street building a day earlier.

"The camera is a good idea. Not much we can do about vandalism unless we catch them in the act," the fresh-faced cop said, adding, "We'll have a report on file."

After the policeman left, we got busy cleaning the sidewalk. I arranged a few of the birch logs and spruce tips that had survived the vandalism. Fido sniffed at the remains of the chaos and ran happily through the sweepings of hay. When we finished, I put him in the truck.

"Guess that will do for now. I'll get another camera and install it, along with more garland and fill-ins for the pots." He surveyed the area.

"Okay."

"When can you do your design magic?" He grinned.

"About four o'clock should work." We hopped in the truck.

"That will give me plenty of time to get the supplies and install the camera. Sure, you don't want to come?" he asked.

"Sorry, I have plans." I squirmed and made a production of brushing Fido's fur from drooping over his eyes.

"Uh huh." Joel gave me a sideways glance and flinched. "Before I forget, I have your check for the work on the apartment." Once home, he parked in his usual spot and slipped the paper from his wallet.

"Thank you," I said, stuffing the payment in my pocket. Just then, Tom Kat leaped out from a hiding spot and pounced at the passenger side door, setting Fido off on a barking spree. I gripped the dog. "You have company," I said, and snickered.

He grinned, and said, "Let him in." Fido and I got out, and the cat jumped into the cab. Joel waved and drove off, with Tom Kat watching through the window.

"Crazy cat is almost like a dog," I muttered while Fido whined.

It was nearly one o'clock, and I hurried to leave for my meeting with Theodore at a nearby coffee shop. Arriving slightly out of breath, I ordered at the counter. Out of the corner of my eye, I spotted a handsome man seated, sipping a beverage from a mug. It had to be Theodore. He was alone, absorbed in his paper, and I hesitated, checked the time, and approached his table.

"Are you Theodore?"

He put the paper aside, smiled, and stood. "You must be Merry."

"Yes."

"Good to meet you. Please sit." He gestured to the chair.

I sat and inhaled. Theodore was perfect. Tall. Mellow voice. Cleft chin, deep brown eyes, and eyelashes any woman would be proud to have.

"Sorry. I wasn't watching. I got involved in reading about the latest Reindeer activities." He gestured to the paper.

"No problem." I cleared my throat. "Can I call you Ted?"

"I prefer Theodore." His lazy brown eyes held a spark of disdain. "In my line of work, people don't take you seriously if you use a nickname."

"Okay." I shifted and laughed nervously. "I hope this isn't work."

"We'll see." He raised his brows and chuckled.

"Aunt Liz said you were a lawyer. What kind of law?" I sipped my coffee, enchanted by his appearance.

"Corporate law. I negotiate deals, advise clients of their rights and duties under the law. Mostly, I prepare legal documents." He sat back, lifted his chin, and asked casually, "What kind of work do you do?"

"I'm between jobs." I sipped my coffee and wrinkled my nose, and added, "The company I worked for was bought out and they downsized."

"You are unemployed?" He sniffed.

"I'm restyling rentals while I look." I cleared my throat.

"Restyle? Like what? Cleaning, painting? That sort of thing?" His eyes narrowed, and his eyes drifted from my navy hoodie to my good blue jeans. His shirt looked expensive, and his jeans were a designer brand.

"Whatever is needed to get the best price on the rental market." I met his gaze. His eyes had clouded over in disapproval.

"Uh, huh? So, you must be in a hurry?" He gestured to my paper coffee cup, shifted his chair away from me, and adjusted his long legs.

"What do you mean?" I blinked and squirmed.

He pointed to his mug.

"A *proper* mug means you plan to stay for a while. It is civilized." Sniffing, he added, "You have a 'to go' cup."

"Oh! You know." Checking the time, I jumped to my feet. "I do need to be someplace. It was nice meeting you, Theodore." My face flushed.

"Uh, huh." He nodded. "Same here, Merry."

Grabbing my 'to go' cup, I dashed for the door, grumbling, "Can't wait to talk to Aunt Liz about this guy."

By the time I got home, I had calmed down. My rant with Aunt Liz could wait. I leashed Fido, who was deliriously happy at the prospect of a hike. We walked along the river walk, under the bridge, and over to the Ivy Lane building where Joel worked. I wanted to check on his progress.

"You're back," he said. "That didn't take long." He descended the ladder, where a new camera hung over the entrance.

"Nope." I tossed my head. "Looks like you've made progress with the display. Good job." I smiled.

"Just in time to do your magic with the decorations." He straightened and gazed at the front. "I'll test the camera."

"Sounds good." I tethered Fido to a small bush while I replicated the outdoor design. He sniffed at the base of the shrub, happy to find unfamiliar scents. Then Tom Kat sauntered from around the corner of the building. His tail was high, and he tiptoed to where Fido sniffed. The dog stiffened, brought up his snout, and met Tom Kat's nose. He took in the cat's scent and waited. Tom Kat reared up, swished his tail, and walked away. Fido looked after him, curious, then went back to sniffing the bush.

I had watched the two, my nerves on edge, then exhaled. "Looks like there's a truce."

Joel had been watching the pair from the front lawn while I worked on the display.

"Tom Kat isn't so bad." He chuckled. "Camera works." He looked up from his cell phone display and gave a slow whistle.

"That looks brand new, nearly better than the original. I would say we are a shoo-in for the festival prize money."

"Thanks; I hope you're right." I collected the remnants of the decorations. "And that there's no more vandalism." Glancing at him, I shrugged, resolute.

"They make the announcement on Black Friday, the day after Thanksgiving. It kicks off the season," he said.

"Wow. It's already the middle of November. It is coming fast. Any plans for Thanksgiving?" I had blurted without thinking, and I added, "Holidays are quiet. Fido and I will go to my Aunt Liz's home."

"Same here. I'll spend the day with my aunt and uncle."

"Your parents are gone?" I asked, hesitating, while gathering the tools and unused supplies.

"Yep. They died when I was in my teens. My aunt and uncle raised me." He shrugged. "What about your parents?" He tilted his head.

"Car accident. My Aunt Liz took me in."

"Yeah. That's kind of the same here." He nodded. His eyes dimmed, cleared his throat, and asked, "Is that the lady who takes Fido some afternoons? Big laugh. I hear her talking to the dog in the hallway."

I viewed him, my brows raised.

"She giggles and swoops in on the dog. He loves it." He laughed.

"Yes. That is Aunt Liz." I grinned.

"Seems like a nice lady."

"She is a great lady. I should get home," I said.

He looked up at the sun low in the sky and checked his watch. "Do you want a lift?"

"No. There's still some light. We will take the river walk home. Before long, we won't be able to get out and enjoy the weather. It is a gorgeous time of year with the scent and colors of the season."

"It is. Enjoy your walk with Fido." He paused while getting into the cab of his truck. "Thanks for coming back and fixing the container." His blue eyes were bright, and his dimples were on full display.

"You're welcome." My heart swelled with warmth, and I waved as he drove away. I lingered along the walkway and sat for a few minutes on a bench that faced the river and watched the rushing water, hypnotized. Fido leaped up and sat next to me. I draped my arm around him, inhaled the scent, and grinned at the reds and golden colors of fall foliage. As darkness fell, we headed home.

Joel

I couldn't believe someone would stoop so low as to trash our displays. It was a nasty blow; who and why would someone do that? It could have been some juvenile prank. Lord knows, I did my share as a teenager. Maybe it was payback for my youthful antics. One time, I had been a punk and tipped over garbage containers and tied cans to cars for a kick. Stupid stuff. The cops caught me and scared me straight with the threat of being locked up in juvenile hall. They gave me a break when they learned my parents were dead.

Thank goodness Merry helped put things back together. Just having her around made the situation tolerable. I was happy when she returned to help with the displays. But is there someone else and if so, who?

If there *is* someone, I can't blame the guy. When she came to the door, her hair was all mussed, and she wore that soft velvet robe. I was sorry she'd changed for shopping. That vision of her, still sleepy, and warm from bed makes me smile. It makes me want to reach out and hold her, but I have to refrain. We have a business arrangement.

When she came back this afternoon, she wore a hoodie that brought out the blue-green color of her eyes. Her hair was soft and flowing. She looked like she had been on a date, but it was a little early in the day. She must have guys dropping at her feet. But she hasn't spoken of any other man. Ahh, she is mysterious; it's like catnip.

Chapter 19

Merry

I WAS READING THE paper, drinking my second cup of java, and perusing the home section when Aunt Liz called Sunday morning, "How was your coffee date with Theodore?"

"Good grief." I sighed. "It wasn't a date."

"Okay? What happened?" Her usual bouncy tone lowered.

"He's arrogant," I protested, remembering his disdainful nod at my paper cup.

"Hmm. He *is* a very successful attorney." Her tone chiding.

"He is self-satisfied and smug. It doesn't matter what kind of work he does," I retorted.

"Julia says he's quite a looker, too," she said. "Handsome."

"Yes. He is, and he knows it." My voice was flat. "I'm sure he has women swooning all the time." Hesitating, I added, "Aunt Liz, please don't fix me up anymore. I know your heart is in the right place, but I can't do it right now."

"Okay." She gave a long sigh. "I know it hasn't gone well, but look at it this way. You are putting yourself out there, and one step closer to finding Mr. Right. Give yourself credit for trying. Can you do that?"

"All right. But no more," I warned.

"We can take a break. Not a long one, mind you. Just a little time out. You will not be twenty-six for long. I want you to find a good husband and father material."

"Okay," I relented. "A break. And I get to say when we're on again." I wanted a committed relationship. Just because Derrick had not worked out, it shouldn't mean the end of a solid partnership for me. My mind wandered to Joel while Aunt Liz chattered. *He would never comment on my cup and had not been judgey about my job woes. When he looked at me, the sparkle in his eyes said he approved, no matter what I wore. Better yet, he liked my apartment design ideas. No allergies and no pink Cadillac. Okay, Fido was still iffy.*

"Absolutely." Aunt Liz broke through my reverie. Her voice hinted at mischief, and I exhaled. She would do what she thought was best. She had always been that way, backing off in the moment, but it would not be long before she had another prospect.

"How's the job search going?"

"Not the best," I admitted. "I have some resumes out there. I have picked up some work with Joel, the building manager here. He saw my apartment and thought I had a good eye for colors and refreshing the vacancies here."

"That's perfect!"

"He entered the buildings in the decorating category for the Reindeer Holiday Festival. I'm helping him with that. There is prize money involved."

"Don't worry about your job search. Things will come together. Wouldn't it be wonderful if you found a whole new career in design instead of the dreadfully dull accounting that you do?" Aunt Liz had a whimsical side to her with a happier vision that made me hopeful.

"That would be awesome."

"Besides, you and Fido can always live with me if something doesn't come through?" Her lilting voice ended on a high note.

"You are sweet, Auntie. I appreciate the invitation. Everything will come together; it won't come to that." I loved Aunt Liz, and I had stayed with her for six months after the Derrick fiasco. I was grateful, but I did not want a reminder, or a repeat of the dark days when I had been too broken to do more than go to work, take care of Fido, then go back to bed. She had been unfailingly cheerful, but it had worn on her too. At the end, she reluctantly agreed that it was best that we have our own space and helped find the pet-friendly building on Holly Street.

"You are coming for Thanksgiving?"

"I would not miss it. I'll bring the mashed potatoes and the pecan pie."

"Great. One o'clock?"

"I'll be there with Fido."

"Of course," she trilled with a giggle.

I spent the days before Thanksgiving on my job search. It appeared the world had taken the week off, with no one returning calls or emails.

I took a breather one evening and called Kris, curious about her new job.

"Hi, Merry!" She sounded buoyant. "How are you?"

"Good. Just curious about the new job. How is it going?"

"It's okay." She sounded distant.

"What's going on?" I asked, puzzled by her tone.

"It's just that...that I think Mr. Bigg has some kind of connection to TREM."

"Total Real Estate Management? The big bad wolf of real estate companies?"

"Actually"—she gave a hearty laugh—"the sharks."

"Oh, yeah." I sighed. "Sharks."

"Keep this to yourself, but I think Mr. Bigg is getting ready to buy more buildings. Maybe even your building on Holly Street, and the sister building on Ivy Lane."

"Oh, no!" I gasped. "If Mr. Bigg and TREM are partners, and they buy this building, it will be the end of pet-friendly, laundry, decent garbage, lawn, and snow services, plus a huge rent increase. Did you hear something?"

"Benjamin has been meeting with Mr. Bigg in his office."

"Not at the new company office?"

"No. It is weird. They clam up when I'm nearby. His office is next to mine."

"You have an office? Nice."

"Yes. It is nice. Before, Mr. Bigg would always see Benjamin at his new location, and now Benjamin is coming to our space. It just seems strange." Her voice trailed off, and she paused.

"Maybe Benjamin is jumping ship and is going to work for Mr. Bigg."

"Maybe," she speculated. "Benjamin could manage Mr. Bigg's buildings and collect rents as an employee. That way, Mr. Bigg wouldn't need to pay an outside company to manage the rentals until he sells them."

"Especially if Mr. Bigg buys up properties to manage himself instead of brokering the deals for TREM."

"Yes. Anyway, it is all hush-hush. The minute Benjamin steps into the workplace, they whisk him off to Mr. Bigg's private office. Benjamin gives me the creeps. I was happy to leave that job."

"Let me know if you hear anything more about my building being sold."

"Will do." We hung up after exchanging 'Happy Thanksgiving' wishes.

Chapter 20

Merry

THE DAY OF THANKSGIVING was cool and sunny, with no snow in sight. I toted my dishes to the car, then returned to my apartment to get Fido. With the dog in tow, I stopped in the entry, where Joel stood on a ladder changing a bulb.

"Leaving for your aunt's house for dinner?" he asked. We had not spoken in a couple of days, and I missed seeing him and his cat.

"Yes. And yourself?" He looked especially handsome in his work jeans and blue-plaid flannel shirt. The scent of woodsy aftershave drifted towards me in the cramped entry.

"Dinner is at four. I'm saving my appetite." He grinned. "So, the Festival judging starts tomorrow at ten o'clock. They announce the big winner at noon sharp, outside city hall."

"Wouldn't it be awesome to win?" I flushed with excitement. "I'll be there."

"Let's go together. And yes. It would." He grinned.

"Okay." I flushed at the invitation.

"It's a plan." Finished with his chore, he stepped down and stroked Fido's head. The dog sniffed his hand. "Probably smells Tom Kat. He is sleeping off his night of prowling as we speak." He turned to me with an appreciative gaze. "You look very nice."

"Thanks." I had fallen into a deep, restful sleep the night earlier, and my hair had behaved that morning after a brisk brushing. I felt my blush deepen at his compliment. "Are all the apartments filled now?"

"Yep. The unit we, *you,* redesigned, was snapped up. The other tenants decided to stay put through the winter." He straightened and met my gaze.

"That's good." Kris's warning echoed in my mind that they could sell the buildings, and I ventured, "So, no big changes in sight?"

"Nope." He grinned.

"Good." Fido tugged at the leash, eager to leave. "Happy Thanksgiving," I said, and waved.

Joel watched our progress, and said, "Happy Thanksgiving!" He added, with a wink, "Looks like the dog is taking you for a walk." He chortled.

It was like a balm seeing Joel, however brief. He was warm and comfortable, like a hug. Relief flooded me, hearing that there weren't any big changes. Energized, I started my car, made a stop at the grocery store, picked up a bouquet of fall flowers for the table, then headed for Aunt Liz's townhouse facing the Reindeer River. She had moved to the new location after her husband, Alvin, passed. They were easily the size of a generous sized single-family home, but were called villas, with an HMO that took care of the lawn and snow.

I loaded my arms with the food dishes and met Aunt Liz at the door. Behind her, I saw two guests standing together at the large window, watching the river churn and gurgle.

"You remember Sophia?" Aunt Liz asked. Sophia was a small, dark- haired, sixty-something woman.

"Yes. Of course." *How could I forget Nico, her son? Allergies.*

Aunt Liz turned to a tall, heavy-set, gray-haired woman. "And Julia is new to the knitters. This is Merry, my niece."

"Nice to meet you." I nodded. "I will get Fido. Be right back." I hustled back to the house with the dog and a bunch of asters, sedum, and goldenrod flowers.

Julia spied the flowers, sniffed, and turned up her nose. "Nice flowers."

I hesitated and handed the bouquet to Aunt Liz, where she scooped them up. "They are beautiful! Thank you!"

"I'll help you get ready." I followed Aunt Liz to the kitchen, where she unbundled the flowers, snipped the ends, and placed them in a crystal vase. She whispered, "Don't mind Julia; her husband is spending the holiday with his mistress in Aspen skiing. She is telling everyone he's traveling for business."

"Oh, my." I gasped. "How do you know?"

"Sophia cued me in." She winked, and her mouth puckered with a snort.

Just then, Sophia called from the formal dining room. "I made napkins just for this occasion! I'll put them out."

"That'd be wonderful!" Aunt Liz called. She finished arranging the flowers and placed them on the food-laden table.

I admired the china and silver and blinked when I saw my place setting. Sophia, as was her nature, had embroidered names with her sewing machine on tan cloth napkins.

"It's M-e-r-r-y," I spelled, "like in Christmas, not M-a-r-y." I had spent my life spelling my name, and it was automatic.

"Sophia," Aunt Liz chided, "you know how to spell her name." She rolled her eyes. "It's Merry. Her mother loved the season."

"Well, I can't keep up with the strange spellings of names these days," Sophia protested. She headed to the counter where a large bottle of white wine and crystal stemware awaited. She uncorked the bottle and poured. "Wine, anyone?"

"Yes. Everyone take a glass and have a seat." Aunt Liz added, "Bring the bottle."

I was the last to pour a glass and placed the wine bottle on the table and took a chair next to Aunt Liz.

"Let's start the food already! I am famished," Aunt Liz announced.

We passed the dishes of green beans, mashed potatoes, gravy, and stuffing around. Aunt Liz carved the turkey. After everyone had served themselves, Aunt Liz clicked her wineglass with a spoon and asked, "What is everyone grateful for this year? Julia, how about you?"

Julia frowned and said, "I'm grateful I'm not looking for a job or a mate." She smirked.

I tensed.

Sophia asked, "How is your job search going, Merry? Aunt Liz told us about your company downsizing. It is terrible they did this right before the holidays."

"That's business. The job search is fine," I said lightly and fingered my wine glass, my appetite dwindling.

"Merry is using her design talent redoing apartments now," Aunt Liz said. "You wouldn't know that. We haven't gotten together for a while." She shot Sophia and Julia cool looks. "Her building manager hired her to do their Reindeer Festival displays as well."

"Well, that's wonderful!" Sophia said.

"Huh!" Julia retorted and stabbed a piece of turkey.

"It's been a welcome change," I said. "What kinds of projects are you doing now?" Getting blank looks around, I looked at Aunt Liz, questioning. "This is part of a knitting club, right?"

"We've expanded our scope," she said, and chuckled.

"Yes!" Sophia agreed. "We go to concerts and any fun events that catch our attention. We are heading to the opening of the festival tomorrow. The shops are having Black Friday specials, and we are going to buy local!"

"Sounds like fun. It is too bad your husband has to work over the holidays, Julia." I added, "Aunt Liz filled me in," and gave her a tight smile.

"Yeah. That's business." She frowned. "How is your love life? My godson, Theodore, said you met for coffee."

Darn. I should have kept quiet.

"Yes, we did. He is very handsome." I stifled a sigh.

"Yes. And very successful. He would be a good catch for any woman." Her tone was lofty.

I heard a clank of dishes from the designated pet food station. "I think Fido needs water. Excuse me." I hurried away, grateful for the distraction. I overheard the women murmuring at the table, comments on the food, and whispers while I attended to Fido. Aunt Liz came up behind me while I dallied at the sink.

"I told them to knock it off," she said. "It is the season of giving thanks. Hug?"

"Thanks." She threw her arms around me, and I said, "Sometimes the holidays bring out the worst in people."

"True." She nodded. "Let's cut the pie."

I cut the pecan pie and offered whipped cream or à la mode. Most opted for whipped cream. Julia was the outlier with heated à la mode.

As time dragged on with the group, Julia finally looked at her watch. "Time to go; husband will be calling." Sophia followed soon after. "Wonderful to see you again, Merry. You have to join our knitters club."

I smiled, my lips firmly pressed, and said, "Nice to see you, too." After she left, I turned to Aunt Liz. "I hope you don't spend every outing discussing my life with your friends."

"I am sorry, Merry. Their lives are dull. They need to hear about something fresh and exciting, like your life." I frowned. "So, the Festival announces the winners of the best holiday design tomorrow! You must be thrilled!"

"I'm nervous," I admitted. "But it will be fun. We worked hard to do a grand design and there were challenges with keeping vandals away."

"Did you ever find out who did the damage?" she asked.

"No." I shrugged. "After Joel put up the cameras, it stopped."

"Good."

"I can hardly wait to hear who wins," Aunt Liz trilled. "It's an honor to be in the competition."

"We can't wait, either," I said, flushing with Aunt Liz's enthusiasm. The image of working alongside Joel brought his calm presence to mind, along with a flash of his dimpled smile.

Chapter 21

Merry

"Merry! Merry!" My eyes flew open. Groggy, I looked at the time on the digital clock. Six o'clock. A.M. Frowning, I listened for a few moments and then heard more pounding, "Merry!" It was Joel.

I threw on my robe and hustled to the entry. Scooping up a barking Fido, I opened the door. Joel hesitated when he saw my disheveled appearance, and the dog squirming in my arms. He ruffled his hair, frustrated.

"Sorry to wake you. The danged delinquents trashed the displays overnight!"

"No!" I inhaled, wide awake now. "How, who?"

"Don't know who. They broke the cameras, and the internet was down. It didn't send the footage to the cloud. If we hurry, we can redo the displays before the judging. The judges will go to the buildings, but I need your help."

"How bad is it?" I looked at him, wide-eyed.

"We can salvage some, but it's going to be a nightmare at The Home Store with Black Friday shoppers to get supplies and then back to fix the displays."

"OMG! I'll feed Fido and meet you at the truck." Springing into action, I dressed in record time, fed Fido, and dashed out. Joel waited in his truck, heater on full blast. I hopped into the cab, and we sped off. We circled the lot, already filled with shoppers. Groaning, I said, "I'll get out while you park and meet you in the seasonal section."

"Sounds good."

I paced impatiently behind a group of people heading into the store. Pouncing at the last cart, I weaved around couples and die-hard bargain hunters, and maneuvered the cart to the area. I hadn't seen the entry to our building because I had taken the back door to the parking lot to Joel's truck. Not sure what was still viable, I plucked out everything. An elderly woman balked when I tugged at the last of the spruce tops from the container.

"I'm desperate!" I said and sent her a pleading look.

She relented, "Go ahead. I don't need them that badly."

"Thank you." I breathed. Joel came up behind me and surveyed the contents.

"Nice haul. Pumpkins and straw bales are outside the store. I will get a few more garlands and more lights. That should do it."

"I'll get in line while you do that." I viewed the check-out line that was forming around the perimeter of the store.

"Take my card." He stuck out a credit card, and I felt a spark from his touch and a surge of warmth as I palmed it. "I'll find you."

"Thanks!" Frantic, I made a determined jaunt to the back of the line. The procession moved slowly, and while shifting from one foot to another, I craned my head to see the cashier. Finally, reaching the register, I unloaded my haul. Scanning the crowd, I searched for Joel's jacket and discovered too many brown jackets to count. As the cashier started ringing up the items, Joel slipped in beside me and added his bounty to the rest, telling the clerk to add the outdoor items to the bill. The elderly fellow behind us in line gave a weary sigh.

"Sorry, man," Joel said.

The gentleman shrugged and said, "No problem. I got all day to wait."

We checked out, and I handed Joel his card as we hurried to the exit.

"How're we doing for time?" I asked as we stopped at the outdoor display to load the bales and pumpkins.

"It's seven-thirty. It will be tight." Then he held up his hand for a high-five. "We got this!" He started jogging with the cart. Laughing, I matched his gait.

The traffic was stop and go as we made our way to the exit; daylight had broken over the horizon. I breathed easier. At least we could see our progress while we reworked the displays.

"Ivy Lane first," Joel said. "We'll do Holly Street last."

"Sounds good." He parked on the street in front of the building, and we gawked at the wreckage. With garbage bags in hands, we hurried cleaning up the mess. While I swept the final debris into the bags, Joel started unloading the new decorations.

I flew into action, recreating the displays and placing items in the containers. Joel pulled an aluminum ladder from the truck bed and tore down remnants of the old and hung the new garland and lights. With lightning speed, I finessed the display, and he descended the ladder.

"Not bad!" Joel draped his arm around me, and I melted at the warmth of his touch.

"Thanks. We might win." The display was fresh and inviting, with the scent of pine wafting from the boughs.

"We're gonna win," Joel said, determined. "I'll come back after the judging to set up another camera."

"Hmm. Whoever it was knew how to damage the camera without being seen."

"Yeah. Not sure what to do about that. It was dark too," he said.

"Is there some sort of alarm that could be attached?"

"I'll look into it." He frowned, checking his watch. "We'd better get home. It is nine o'clock!"

We hustled to the truck and headed to Holly Street, where we redid the display. Breathless, with six minutes to spare, we stood back, satisfied.

"It's beautiful," Joel said in awe. "Another high five!" I matched his hand with mine as snowflakes fell and gazed up at him. He was tired, but happy. The heat from his body felt soothing. My stomach melted at his peaceful, satisfied expression. We had done it together.

"There are the judges," I said, watching a van labeled Reindeer Festival park in front of the building. "I'll get rid of this stuff." Scooping up the trowel and gloves, I headed inside.

"Come back for the photo op!" Joel called.

Waving him off, I ran upstairs. After depositing the items on my table, I hurried to the bathroom to check my hair and makeup.

"Aawk!" I was a mess, with dirt on my face and hair in disarray. After a quick swipe of my face with a cloth, I slapped on lip gloss and ran a brush through my hair. Dashing back, Fido's angry barks echoed as I ran down the hall.

The judges, a man and a woman, carried clipboards and marked items as they examined the newly refurbished presentation. When all the paperwork was completed, they took photos of the display, and then of Joel and me standing in front of the decorated entry.

"You have the building on Ivy Lane, too?" the woman asked. "You don't have to be present at each location."

"Wouldn't miss it," Joel said. "We'll see you there." He grabbed my hand, and we headed to his truck and drove back to Ivy Lane. I felt shy with the feel of his hand, not sure what was happening between us, and sneaked peeks at his profile while he drove; I felt the invisible wall I had, slip.

"Thank goodness, it's still in one piece!" I exclaimed as we reached the display.

"You know it!" He grinned.

Snow fell in big fluffy flakes, and we threw the hoods up on our coats, watching the frosting effect on the garland and the pumpkins.

"They'd better hurry," I said.

"Here they are," Joel said as the van pulled up; the couple got out and took notes.

"Ready for another photo?" the man asked.

"Sure." Joel threw his arm around my shoulders, and we grinned for the camera.

"We will announce the winner at noon in front of the courthouse," the man said.

"We'll be there." Joel looked down at me, a question in his expression.

"Of course we will," I said.

"You two make a cute couple. Good luck," the woman with the clipboard said, smiling.

Couple!

Impulsively, I teased, fluffing my hair, and fluttering my lashes at Joel, blushing. His expression went blank as he drove home, and we headed to the safety of our apartments.

Inside, his back against the door, his eyes darting from my gaze, he said, "I'll stop by a few minutes before noon. It was a good morning. Thanks again for all your help, Merry." My stomach dropped; it had become awkward between us. I felt silly. Was I imagining something from him that wasn't there?

***

When Joel knocked later. I was ready to go, with my coat and a scarf wrapped around my neck, and gloves in hand. I hurried out of the apartment, locking it.

"Are you nervous?" he asked as we trekked the three blocks to the courthouse. The snow had collected an inch, and we shuffled through, our shoes getting soggy.

"Yes." I sneaked another look at him and felt my stomach surge.

"Don't be. It is just money." He grinned.

"It might mean commissioned work for me." I had channeled Aunt Liz while waiting, pacing inside, playing fetch with Fido, and biting my nails, pondering what had gone amiss with Joel.

We stood in the covered entry of the courthouse downtown and waited for the announcement from the festival organizers. A small group had assembled, and we looked at each other warily, awaiting the announcement. Few smiled; most gritted their teeth and looked at their feet, or shifted, hands stuffed in pockets. I wondered if anyone there had a hand in destroying our décor overnight.

"The winners of this year's festival decorating design are Joel Connor and Merry Ernst for their Winter Wonderland displays!"

We gasped. I jumped up and down, clapping my hands. On impulse, I leaned up to kiss Joel's cheek. He turned and caught my lips, leaving a soft, firm kiss. My toes curled, and my stomach warmed.

The crowd cheered and clapped. Grinning, we stood on the steps shoulder to shoulder while the couple who had taken notes at the displays handed us a huge replica of the $10,000 check.

"Congratulations, Joel and Merry!"

"What are you going to do with the money?" A young male reporter from the weekly paper asked.

"Pay my rent!" I spoke. The audience laughed.

"It will go to the owners for repairs and for good use around the building. They are proud of the apartment homes they provide for the citizenry of Reindeer and want to do the best job possible for the community," Joel said.

The man looked at me quizzically, laughing. "He charges you rent?"

"We're not married," Joel said. "We're friends." He squeezed my hand. "Good friends."

My heart sank. "Yes, friends." I felt my barrier slide up and lock in place.

"Uh huh," the emcee said. "We'll get the real check to you the next business day, this Monday."

We walked back to Holly Street in silence. The snow had picked up, and a wind whipped snowflakes in our faces as we trudged. I left Joel on the first floor, and he detoured to the back of the building while I headed to the staircase.

"I'll stop by with your part of the prize money as soon as I have it," he said as we parted ways.

"Sure." Nodding, I took the stairs to my apartment.

"Thanks again, Merry. You did a fabulous job." His cheeks dimpled.

"You're welcome." Wearily, I stepped into the hall and trudged to my door. *We are just friends.* My back stiffened with resolve, and I greeted Fido with an enormous hug. "Thank goodness, I have you." I whispered into his fur.

Joel

Merry was pure dynamite when she worked on those displays. My breath caught, seeing her enthusiasm and near panic at the devastation of the vandals. She was fierce, her face reflecting her determination to get the jobs done at record speed. I wanted the money for us, but she was a tiger. It scared me. This woman could be the one, but I'm not ready for anything more than 'friends.' She had teased, but I felt her stiffen, her resistance at the prize announcement, and an alarm went off. Did she feel something more for me? Or was I misreading her?

I felt guilty at not being straight with her about the ownership of the buildings, but the Goldmans gave me a chance to manage the buildings, to earn my stripes in keeping the residences in good stead. I did not want to blow it by getting involved with a tenant, even a cute one with a feisty dog. Even though I didn't owe her any explanation, she was getting under my skin. I wanted to tell her everything about everything.

Chapter 22

Merry

Saturday morning, I bundled up and leashed Fido. We went outside for the morning ritual. Joel had plowed the parking lot, and we visited the cleared area. I deposited the baggie and hurried back up.

While removing my coat, the phone rang, and frowning at the number, I answered.

"How are you, honey bunny?" the tenor voice came.

"Derrick?" It startled me hearing the old nickname.

"You remember!" He chuckled.

"Oh, Derrick. I couldn't ever forget you," I snipped. "Why are you calling?"

"It's the holidays, honey. I wanted to say happy holidays and see how you are."

"I'm not your honey." Silence. "Did something happen to my replacement?" I demanded. Until I heard his voice, I did not realize how much anger I had toward Derrick for how he'd treated me.

"I am sorry, Merry. I know I hurt you, and I was a Class A jerk."

"Worse than that!" I snapped. "Liar and a cheat!"

"I've changed." He was quiet. "I would like to prove that to you. If you are free, I would like to take you to lunch." Wheedling, he added, "It *is* the season of forgiveness."

The tone of his voice got through, and I relented. "We can be cordial. Friends." That miserable word.

"Friends could work." He chuckled. "I would like that. I want to make it up to you for the garbage I put you through."

"One o'clock. Lunch." I was firm.

"I'll pick you up."

"You know where I live?" My shoulders tensed.

"Yes. I got your address from your aunt. She is a gem."

That would be my next call. What was she thinking? I hung up, exasperated, determined to tell Aunt Liz not to give out my personal information. She had tagged him as a loser, too. I hung up when my call went to voicemail. Upon reflection, I realized she knew it was me and didn't want to talk, and her happy-ever-after gear had likely kicked in. I calmed myself with the idea that it was best to have closure with Derrick and face him one last time.

I dressed in black. Black jeans, turtle-neck sweater, and coat. It fit my mood. Ready to go, I opened the door to his knock, holding Fido back.

Derrick was rail thin, six feet tall, with a dark brown shock of hair. He wore a neat, trimmed beard. His dark brown eyes glowed, and they had once fascinated me with their charm. Now, not so much. He looked down at me over a beak of a nose, his mouth twisted in a grin.

"You look great, Merry." He gave a nervous chuckle.

"You look the same. I'll get my purse," I said and shut the door in his face. No, I would not let him in. The thing that had impressed me about Derrick was he loved to talk to women. If we weren't together, we would talk on the phone for hours. Time would escape us. I had never met a man who enjoyed talking on the phone like he did. I put it down to the fact he was smack dab in the middle between four sisters, no brothers. He knew how to talk to females. When he spent time on the phone while we were married, he claimed it was with one of his sisters. Until he couldn't lie any longer.

We were both in college when we met via the dating site. I worked to pay rent and qualified for college aid and loans. His family had the means to pay his way. That would end if he married before he finished school. My company took me on full time, and I took one night class a semester. It was supposed to be for one year.

I had married him with lingering doubts after I learned he came from a solid upper middle-class family that lived in a wealthy suburb, with a father who was the sole supporter of the family, complete with a stay-at-home doting mother. When I contrasted my upbringing with Aunt Liz, who worked the overnight shift as a nurse to support the two of us after her husband died, and no huge family support system, I felt lacking. His mother had the same twisted smirk that Derrick had, and I felt 'less than' for her only son.

"How about Mexican? I am tired of turkey," he added. He took my elbow and guided me down the hall and out to his Honda Civic. We buckled up, and he asked, "El Mexicano?"

"Sounds good."

We ordered drinks and food at the grill and ate chips and salsa while making small talk.

"How's your mother?" I asked.

"She still serves lunch on china dishes with cloth napkins." He chuckled. I remembered the first time I met her. Lunch was finger sandwiches on Wedgewood China with pink cloth napkins.

"And your sisters?"

"Oh. They came with their spouses and children and mobbed the parents' house over Thanksgiving. It was mayhem. I had a headache by the time I left."

"How was your Thanksgiving?" he asked.

"Fine." I was short, reluctant to share any details of my life.

"You look great," Derrick gushed.

"You said that." My eyes narrowed, and I studied his geeky appearance. He had never been comfortable in jeans and a sweatshirt. He wore a sweater over a buttoned-down shirt collar now and khakis. Once, I had found the look endearing. Now, he looked haggard, with dark circles under his eyes, masked by heavy, black-rimmed frames. The words slipped out. "You look tired." My mouth puckered.

He nodded. "Sarah moved out. She claimed she was sick and couldn't come to dinner at the parents. I came home to an empty house and her clothes gone."

You know what they say about karma.

"Sorry." I was sorry, but not that sorry.

"So, who's moving in?" I snipped and sipped my Coke.

"No one," he mumbled. "I goofed, Merry. I messed up bad." He sounded sincere. "I miss you." Gazing, he held my eyes with his and asked, "Are you seeing anyone?"

"We agreed to be friends, right?" I said, tense. That word again, friends.

"It's a start." He grinned. "I learned from being with Sarah what I really needed in a relationship. She was not good for me. Clingy. You were never clingy."

"I don't need to know details," I said and snapped a chip between my fingers. *Yeah. She knew she couldn't trust you.*

"I married you. I did not marry Sarah." He reached across the table for my hand. I withdrew.

He straightened and leaned his back against the wooden booth. The waiter left our entrees, mine a taco salad, his a burrito. We reached for our utensils.

"So, you're between jobs?" he asked and sliced into the soft shell.

"Yes. I helped redesign an apartment in my building while I search for permanent full-time."

"You were always ambitious, a worker. You liked art." He smiled. My shoulders sagged, and I forked a piece of lettuce.

"How's your job?" Derrick had scored a high-paying job with the help of his father's influence.

"Downsizing. It is the word of today about companies. Do more, with less, and all of that." He grimaced. "They haven't found me yet."

"Yeah. They found me." I laughed for the first time.

"You don't seem too upset." He peered at me.

"I want to be a designer, work with colors and spaces."

"Well, then. I think you will." His smile was wide. "I'm sure of it."

"Thank you." I hesitated. "Joel and I won the Reindeer Festival's holiday decorating challenge.

"Who's Joel?" he asked, his sharp brown eyes piercing.

"He's the building super." I flushed.

"You seem happy. You glow when you talk about this Joel fellow." He studied me, about to swallow a forkful of food, and squinted.

"He's become a friend." My cheeks were hot with color. "We won the contest. We are splitting the prize money."

"How much?" Derrick, ever the MBA.

"Ten thousand dollars."

"Nice." His brows raised; he sipped his cola. Finished with his entrée, he pushed his plate away. The server darted in to get our dishes.

"It helps," I said and checked the time. "It's nearly two-thirty. I should get back. Fido awaits."

"Ah yes. The dog." Derrick hadn't wanted a dog. He had a cat, Lucy, who had a penchant for eating the collar on my warmest parka. I didn't know the collar had real fur until Lucy shredded it. Lucy and I made our peace by my keeping my parka out of sight. I wanted the companionship of a dog.

I rescued Fido from a local animal shelter after we split up. Aunt Liz loved animals, dogs in particular, so she was enthusiastic about my adopting Fido. The problem had been finding a dog-friendly apartment. When she found the building, we were excited and celebrated with fudge sundaes.

"So, Joel is a friend, besides being the building manager." His voice was low, and he sniffed, rubbing the end of his nose with the side of his index finger. He slipped out his wallet and laid a credit card with the bill.

"Yes." I scooted out of the booth and shrugged into my jacket. The server returned with the receipt and the card. Derrick stretched his long legs from under the booth, stood, and zipped his coat.

We walked to his car in silence. On the drive home, he said, "Merry. I miss what we had. I hope we can become better friends."

It was hard to describe what I felt. We had history. It hadn't always been bad, but I had changed. I squirmed when Derrick parked next to Joel's truck in the parking lot. Joel sauntered from the back entrance, toolbox in hand. Tom Kat rode his shoulder. I slunk down and looked out the passenger's side window. This could be embarrassing.

"Is that him?" Derrick asked. "The super?" His nostrils quivered.

"Uh, huh." I nodded.

Joel stowed his toolbox in the back, opened the driver's side, and Tom Kat leaped into the seat. He drove off without a glance at Derrick's small gray car.

"Looks like an interesting fellow." He chuckled. "Can I come up, use the bathroom?"

I hesitated. "Okay."

Upstairs, I caught Fido, and held him from taking out Derrick's ankle, and waited in the living room.

He entered the living room, and Fido, on guard, barked. Derrick looked nervous.

"He won't bite, will he?"

"Yes. He will. He doesn't like strangers. In fact, Fido doesn't much like anyone else except me." I held back the dog and reprimanded him, "Hush. It is okay."

"I'll sit over here," he motioned to the easy chair. "I'll bring him a toy next time I come." He looked hopefully at me and sat.

"Derrick. I'm pretty busy these days."

"If it works, okay? No pressure. I miss you. I couldn't stop thinking about you, even when Sarah and I were together."

Shaking my head. "Don't do this."

"You're right." He rose quickly. The sudden move sent Fido into another fit of barking. "I'll let you get on with the rest of your day. It was wonderful seeing you again."

"Sure, Derrick." I saw him to the door. He gave a parting salute, turned, and nearly ran into Joel, striding through the hall. No cat.

"Sorry, man." Joel sidestepped Derrick.

"My fault," Derrick said. The two men sized each other up briefly. Derrick left; his nose twitched as he sent a parting glare toward the building manager.

Joel looked at me and asked, "Company, huh?"

"Yes. My ex."

"You're friendly with him?"

"Yes. Well, no. It is a long story," I stammered. I wasn't sure how I felt after seeing Derrick. He was familiar, and that was comfortable.

"I got time." Joel grinned and leaned against the doorjamb.

I shook my head. "Did you want something?"

"Hi, Fido." He reached over to pet the dog. Fido accepted his affection and looked at him expectantly.

"I think he wants to know where Tom Kat is." I chuckled. "Or if you have a treat."

"Left him at home," Joel said. "No treats, buddy." He gazed at me. "Say, I looked through the pictures from the cameras on the displays. What I could retrieve, anyway. There's a blurry image of a face. I wanted to see if you recognized it. But if you are busy?"

"No! I want to see what you have found. Come in!" I stepped aside, and he brushed past, the fresh scent of the outdoors clinging to his clothes.

"I'll put on coffee or tea."

"Cola, if you have it," he said. Slipping off his jacket, he draped it over a chair in the kitchen and sat at the table, scrolling through his phone.

"Yes. It's a Diet Coke," I said, setting down the bottle and a glass.

"Not picky," he said absently. He looked up from his phone. "But I prefer classic Coca Cola, full sugar," and he grinned.

"Duly noted," I said and matched his smile, taking in the flash of a twinkle.

He went back to his phone and scrolled through the video taken by the cameras before someone trashed it. "See, this is it! This is the last scene before the screen went black." He held it up.

I took the phone and squinted at the blurry image and gasped. "That looks like Benjamin!"

"Who's that?" He sipped his drink.

"Benjamin is my old boss. He went to TREM when they bought my company." I frowned. "But Kris said he might jump ship to work for Mr. Bigg now."

"And Mr. Bigg is?" He drawled the question, his brows raised.

"Mr. Bigg is a real estate broker. He puts deals together for investors. Mainly apartment buildings, some commercial buildings too." I scrolled through the images, curious. Dim lighting from the streetlights showed the displays were intact, then a brief image of a man wearing chunky black glasses reaching toward the camera, then all went dark.

"So, Benjamin doesn't own any buildings?"

"Not that I know of."

"Could he have been doing Mr. Bigg's dirty work so he could take us out of the competition for the festival prize money?" Joel asked.

"All I know is that he was adamant about getting mine and Kris's ideas before the new company took over. But then Kris said she saw him in Mr. Bigg's office, and they would clam up whenever she was around. She wasn't sure what his connection was." Frowning, I asked, "Only owners could enter the competition?" I tilted my head, thoughtful.

"I had the Goldmans' permission," Joel said quickly. Red colored his face.

"Then Benjamin could have entered with the owner's permission, too. For TREM, or whomever he works for."

"Maybe." He sounded skeptical. "Thanks, Merry. I wanted your opinion. And thank you again for all your help with the competition. I will install cameras again. I don't think whoever is doing this is done causing mischief."

"We won. Even if they keep it up, the prize money is ours," I said.

"It will be good public relations for the Goldmans. Fewer vacancies, word of mouth of how good it is to live at the Holly Street or Ivy Lane apartments. Not so good, if the vandals keep it up." He frowned, pursing his lips. He slipped the phone into his shirt pocket and turned towards me, viewing my outfit. "You look good in black." He grinned, his head tilted.

"Thanks." I teased, "I think brown is your color." The contrast between Derrick's stylish coat and Joel's work jacket flashed across my mind. *Cut it out.* 'Friends, good friends,' he had told the announcer.

The air was thick, and I realized how close we were at the table. He stood and reached for his jacket on the back of the chair. I took a deep breath and rose, too.

"Thanks for the Coke and the company. I had better get back to it. There is a problem with the dryer in the basement."

"Oh?" I looked sideways at him, admiring his wavy brown locks, and crossed my arms.

"Someone,"—he drawled, and buttoned his coat, clearing his throat—"ran the dryer without the lint trap. I believe there is a sock lodged in the dryer mechanicals now."

"That's where all those socks go!" I laughed.

"That's it!" He grinned and raised his brows, nodding toward the cola. "Mind if I take the bottle?"

I nodded. "Help your se—" Before I finished speaking, he swooped in and planted a soft kiss on my lips. He winked and closed the door behind him. Another kiss? What just happened? My mind whirled, confused, and giddy. My heart sang, and my stomach warmed with the soft touch.

Joel

Dang it, I couldn't help myself. Merry looked so foxy wearing that black sweater. The way her hair flowed and lay on her shoulders in waves and the rosy glow on her cheeks. Her surprise at the photo of Benjamin. I had to kiss her. I need to ask her out, despite what the Goldmans might think. They didn't have to know, did they?

Just who was that ex? If you ask me, the guy looked a little twisted, wearing khakis and sporting a beard. A little too buttoned down for Merry. For an instant, Patricia's face had flashed in my mind when I saw the dude outside Merry's door, and I squelched the pain I felt when she left. What was his deal? Why would an ex visit? For nothing good, that was for sure.

He needed to watch his step. I would be watching.

And Benjamin needed to mend his ways, too. Why was this dude causing problems? There was plenty of business in Reindeer Falls. He didn't have to knock out the competition. He has to compete with good housing.

Chapter 23

Merry

My phone rang, and in a daze, I answered.

"I tried earlier, and there was no response," Aunt Liz said. "I didn't leave a message. Caller ID said you rang." She added in a high, breathy tone, "You sound funny."

I hadn't checked my device. If it was important, whoever it was would leave a message. Aunt Liz made a habit of checking hers.

"Derrick took me to lunch today. He said you gave him my address and phone number." I tried not to sound accusatory.

"No. It wasn't me. You know how I feel about Derrick? Eek!"

"Huh?" I recalled his words, that he "learned it from Aunt Liz," and said, exasperated, "What he probably meant was that he googled your name and address, noted I was associated with you, and followed the crumbs to my information."

"That sounds like Derrick." She laughed. "Skirting the truth. Telling you he talked to his sister but not admitting, he talked to that gal, Sarah, around the same time. Lying by omission."

"Yes. The master of manipulation," I said.

"How was lunch?" she asked.

"Sarah left. He wants to start things up again." I sighed.

"Hmm," she ventured slowly, hesitantly, "How do you feel?"

"Confused. He said he married me, *not* Sarah."

"Sarah didn't put up with his nonsense," she retorted.

"Okay, Aunt Liz," I chided.

"You're a mush; just saying." She laughed. "It's a family trait."

"Enough." I hated she knew me that well. She hadn't given Derrick my information, so she hadn't had a crisis of conscience. It had not been a case of Happy Ever After or let bygones be bygones.

"You are right. I am sorry. I saw the festival winner's announcement on the local news. Congratulations!"

"It was on the news?"

"Yes. You and that maintenance fellow. You make a cute couple." Good grief, nothing like a public display of affection for television viewing.

I groaned.

"Uh, huh. I have to go now," and hung up.

I was curious about Benjamin's status with the company now. It seemed beneath him to vandalize displays. He had been my boss. But he had spouted a motto in a nasal tone of voice, and a long, serious face: *If you want something done correctly, do it yourself.* He had muffed wrecking the displays by showing his face on camera. I called Kris, wanting to know if she had any more intel on Benjamin.

"Merry, I saw you on television with that hot maintenance guy! You won the Reindeer Festival Challenge. Congratulations!" In the same breath, she asked, "Are you two an item?" She gushed, "He's a cutie."

"You heard him. We are friends." I wanted to keep Joel's kiss to myself and hold on to that feeling.

"Huh. Pretty cozy friends," she teased. "What does Fido think of him?"

"He's okay." I had to admit he had accepted Joel. Even he and Tom Kat had a sort of truce.

"How is it going with Mr. Bigg and company?"

"Funny you should ask." Her voice was thoughtful as she spoke. "We worked on Black Friday. Of course, the busiest shopping day of the year is not a real holiday for the bulk of us worker bees." She sighed. "I'd rather be shopping."

"Go on," I urged.

"Benjamin came by that afternoon. He was quiet, almost morose. Mr. Bigg waved him into his office and closed the door."

"Is that any different from the usual?"

"A little. For one, Benjamin usually nods at me. He is not chummy, but he acknowledges me. Second, there were loud voices from Mr. Bigg's office. Mostly, Mr. Bigg's. Somehow, Benjamin screwed up."

"He took our ideas, and he was supposed to win the decorating challenge," I submitted.

"Yep. So, when Mr. Bigg saw you and Joel,"—she harrumphed—"it didn't go well for Benjamin."

"But do you think TREM or Mr. Bigg care about winning a contest?"

"Where there's money involved, Mr. Bigg totally cares!"

"But ten thousand dollars is a drop in the bucket to a man like him."

"It is more about the prestige and convincing the residents of Reindeer that it's a good idea for him to broker more buildings for TREM. Have you seen any of the TREM-owned buildings?"

"One or two, maybe."

"Check out their newest acquisition. It is further down from the Goldman's building on Ivy Lane. They bought it last month, and it is already a mess! They have stopped cleaning the entry and halls, garbage is piling up because they haven't paid the refuse company. It is too cold for people to move now, so every day there are angry tenants calling and complaining."

"And Benjamin is still working for TREM?"

"Yep, he would get the angry calls."

"Do you think Mr. Bigg has a financial interest in TREM?"

"That would make sense, given how often Benjamin shows up."

"Let me know if you hear anything."

"Sure."

"So, are you ready to go online with your dating profile?" she asked. The teasing tone was back.

"Good grief. No!"

"Call me if you change your mind. 'Friends' wouldn't cut it for me with a hot guy like your maintenance fellow."

"You sound like Aunt Liz now," I protested.

"Your aunt is a smart cookie," she said.

"I've got to go."

"Uh huh." Laughing, she hung up.

I disconnected, thinking about Benjamin, his job at TREM, and the vandalism of the displays. Just what was his connection to Mr. Bigg?

I bundled up, put a jacket on Fido and leashed him, and headed to my car. We were going to take a field trip and check out the building that TREM managed on Ivy Lane. Kris had said it was near the building that the Goldmans owned.

When I saw that our display was in pristine condition, I breathed a sigh of relief. Joel had put the camera back up and it made me smile; the display was so cheerful. Continuing down the block, where a few houses were scattered between apartment buildings, I stopped at the corner. A sign in front of the building announced TREM was the new management company.

Kris was right. The building, about the same age as others in the area, looked dismal. Tenants had made a path through light snow into the entry. An overhead lightbulb was out. Curious, I parked, told Fido, "I'll be right back." Locking the car with my spare key, I left the motor running, with the heater on, and tramped through the snow into the building. I scanned the entrance. It was littered with flyers and discarded fast food wrappers, as though residents had given up and went to their homes, ignoring the obvious neglect. Why had Benjamin been so insistent on getting Kris and my ideas if he would not use them?

As I left, a young couple entered the building. They appeared to be twenty-something. The young woman's long dark hair trailed from under a white knit cap with a large pompom. They both wore gold and green jackets with U of MN logos and blue jeans.

"Hi. Do you live here?" I asked.

"Yeah." The young man snorted. "It's a dump."

The young woman agreed, "Sure is."

He looked at me, "Why? Are you looking to rent?"

"Maybe." I didn't want to tell the tenant I was secretly snooping. "I live nearby on Holly Street. This used to be a well-kept building in a wonderful neighborhood. Now, it looks shabby," I said, flinching.

"You don't know the half of it. The garbage dumpster hasn't been emptied in almost a month. There are mice and bugs in the apartments. The new management hasn't done anything since they took over!"

"The residents try to keep the entry and halls clean, but people are fed up," the woman said. "We are moving as soon as we find another place. But we must have first and last month's rent, plus a damage deposit. We've heard that TREM does not return damage deposits, either!"

"We just want our services back, and the place maintained like it used to be. It is a boatload of money to move," he said. "We're students."

"And the holidays are coming!" the woman exclaimed.

"Have you called the city? You can make a complaint about the management. If the company has enough violations, they can lose their rental license."

"Then, that's what we'll do," the young man said, determined. His expression was stoney.

"First thing Monday," the woman agreed. "Hopefully, we won't get kicked out for complaining." She gave the man a worried look.

"If you can get other residents to call too, that would help the cause. Document everything, take pictures," I added.

"Thanks. If we have to move, so be it." He put his arm around her. "They have to give us an eviction notice. First, we'll see if filing a complaint with the city will convince the owners to clean up," the young man said.

"Good luck to you both." I smiled. "Sorry, you have to deal with this mess."

I went back to my car with Fido waiting patiently. "Fido, this place is a disaster." I hoped the young couple and the rest of the residents could once again have a safe, comfortable, and sanitary place to live. I drove away, feeling lucky, knowing Joel wouldn't let the buildings he managed go to seed.

Chapter 24

Merry

PAY DAY

Monday morning at ten o'clock, I sat in front of my computer screen, absorbed in my job search, when a knock sounded at the door. A peek at the security hole showed Joel, with Tom Kat riding his shoulder. I stepped into the hall.

"Hi, I wanted to get this to you asap." He grinned and thrust an envelope at me. "This is your part of the festival winnings."

"Perfect! This will stave off the wolf for a few months." I laughed.

"Good. Because we have a strict 'no wolves allowed' policy at the building!" he deadpanned.

"I'll remember that." Laughing, I viewed Tom Kat perched on his shoulder and took in Joel's lean, well-muscled body, clad in a flannel shirt and work jacket. "I'd invite you in, but you're wearing your cat today."

"Yep, we are heading over to Ivy Lane to check out the display and shovel the sidewalk. Got to plow out, too." A three-inch snowfall had accumulated overnight.

I hesitated and blurted, "I talked to my old co-worker, Kris. She said that TREM had taken over managing a building on Ivy Lane. I was curious, so I drove there. It is a mess—no shoveling, broken light bulbs. The entry is littered with trash. I spoke with a young couple who wanted the building maintained like it had been, but management has brushed them off. I told them to call the city to complain."

"I'm not surprised." He snorted, disgusted. "Poor management affects the entire neighborhood and the value of other buildings. Besides, tenants deserve excellent services."

"Has anyone wanting to buy the buildings approached the Goldmans?"

"There are always people looking to snap up these buildings." He shrugged. "They are not interested."

"Good." I was relieved. In the back of my mind, I had fretted about the Goldmans selling and what that might mean to me and my pet-friendly haven.

Fido whined inside, and Tom Kat raised up to all fours on Joel's shoulders, wary.

"I'll let you go," I said. "Thank you." I held up the envelope. "This means a lot to me."

"You earned it." His dimples deepened.

"It's not only the money, but I can add this to my portfolio for future display work. Winning the grand festival prize money is an honor."

"Sure." He grinned. "I'll be happy to provide a reference along with the Goldmans."

"Thank you."

He added, "Add the holiday touches when you can. We made it through Thanksgiving. No rush." He held his hand up for emphasis.

"Of course! I will go to the bank and change out the displays today."

"I'll leave the items in the entry before I go to Ivy Lane."

"Sounds good." I nodded, winking at Tom Kat, who had snuggled into Joel's neck and rested on his shoulder, then ducked back into my apartment.

My day set, I headed to the bank to make my deposit, then returned to take out the pumpkin and add sprigs of holly berries to the pots. Satisfied with the seasonal touches, I disposed of the pumpkin at the garbage dumpster. I did the same at Ivy Lane, noting with a little disappointment that I had missed Joel and Tom Kat. I snapped pictures of the result and was pleased to see the security cameras in both buildings were intact.

***

At home again, I called Aunt Liz. "I'd like to take you to lunch to celebrate my winnings if you're available."

"I'd love to!" she exclaimed. "You got the money?"

"Yes. Mexican or Panera?" I suggested our two favorite haunts.

"Let's try to eat healthy before the rash of holiday treats. I have no self-control," she said.

"Panera, it is. We will have a healthy celebration. Salads?"

"Yes. Promise you will keep me away from the pastries?"

"Deal!" I laughed.

We met in the restaurant's entry. Aunt Liz carried a small gift bag. She greeted me with a broad smile and hug, and we ordered at the counter.

"This is on me," she said, and took out her wallet.

"No." I argued. "It's my treat! I did not invite you to lunch for you to pay." I thrust the cash toward the counter person who shrugged and took Aunt Liz's credit card.

"I get no respect," I said, and rolled my eyes. "I wanted to treat you."

"Another time." Aunt Liz smiled sweetly. "Let's get our coffee." We found a booth and settled in, waiting for our order. She popped the gift bag in front of me.

"What's this?" I asked. "It isn't my birthday."

"It's for Fido."

"Oh. Well, then I accept." It was a small plaque with a dog, and letters in dominoes, "Top Dog Designer!"

"I love it! He will, too."

"It was a whim. Just something to celebrate your victory. You worked hard to win the prize money."

"We did. And we had the last-minute speed designing, too." I nodded, reflecting on the damaged displays. Remembering the nearly automatic coordination, really a dance, with Joel, righting the pots, reworking the containers, and the satisfaction we had when they were complete.

"You still don't know who's responsible for the damage?" she asked.

"Nope. We can guess. There was a glimpse of Benjamin's face the first time, but nothing more. It will all come out sometime." I sipped my coffee.

"Any word from Derrick?" she asked.

"No." I shook my head. "It bugs me he turned up so quickly after Sarah left."

"Maybe I have been too hasty. Do you think he has changed and grown up since you and he parted?" She was thoughtful.

Our buzzer sounded, and I went to the window to pick up our food and returned to the booth.

"Derrick seemed sincere, but I am guessing it is any port in a storm with him. I don't know if I could see him again." I gulped. "If I could forgive him for being such a rat."

"Maybe he's not the one you need to forgive." She gazed at me.

I studied her, puzzled.

"Maybe you need to forgive yourself. For being with someone who didn't treat you the way you wanted to be treated."

I nodded. My shoulders sagged. "You are right. I feel like I should have known, and that I did something wrong. I was working, busy." Tilting my head, I met her gaze.

"Do you still have feelings for him?" she asked.

Clearing my throat, I sat back, toying with my salad with my fork.

"It was awkward seeing him again, but comfortable. Kind of like the devil, you know, feeling?"

"Ahh." She nodded. "You'll figure it out."

We left the restaurant with more hugs and Aunt Liz's promise to host Christmas dinner as usual, amid my protestations that we would get together before then. The holiday was a few weeks off—plenty of time.

I played my messages at home, grimacing. Speak of the devil.

"Hi, Merry! I saw you in the paper and I wanted to say good job in person. Call me." It was Derrick.

I grumbled about the message. I didn't need his praise. There wasn't any reason to call. Shrugging, I took Fido out. Absorbed in our duties, I retrieved his contribution and looked over at the sidewalk. Derrick, a big grin on his face, watched our progress.

"Did you get my message?" he asked. His dark eyes were bright.

"What are you doing here?" I frowned, startled. "I just got home." *Good grief, he was turning into a stalker.*

"I saw the photo in the paper of you and that man, Joel. You won the decorating contest. Congratulations!"

"Thank you." I relaxed. "You spooked me."

"Sorry," he said. "Didn't mean to." He laughed nervously. "Can I come up? I could use a cup of coffee."

"Okay." I was resigned. My conversation with Aunt Liz had impressed me there wasn't any getting over Derrick's indiscretion. I had to let go of the myth that we could rewrite our history and become a couple again, the myth Derrick was pushing. It was time to move on. I deserved someone I could trust, and it wasn't Derrick. I would have that wall up forever, ever wary of what he could do to my heart again.

He sat at the kitchen table while fresh coffee brewed, and I pondered what to do about his presence in my life again. Was it possible for us to be friends? Could I let that happen?

"Derrick, I've thought about us."

"That doesn't sound good." He frowned, crossed his legs, and studied me, looking down his long nose.

"I think it's best we leave us, as a couple, in the past."

"I see." He frowned and sipped his coffee. "Why?"

"I've changed." Silence hung in the air. He rubbed his nose and sniffed.

"You don't love me."

"It's different." I said finally. "It isn't a couple's kind of feeling. That is gone."

"Friends?" He looked hopeful.

"Maybe." I shrugged, avoiding his stare.

"I really screwed it up, didn't I? Taking up with Sarah?"

"Yes." Wincing, I nodded and felt a part of my wall slip with his acknowledgment of the pain he had caused.

"I'm sorry."

"Thank you."

"Well, if that's how you feel." He set his cup on the table and rose. "I won't keep you any longer."

After I walked him out to the parking lot, then went back up to grab my garbage bag for the week, musing as I headed to the dumpster at how symbolic it was, removing the garbage after Derrick left.

I lifted the lid and threw in the bag; turning, I saw Joel. He and a young woman approached his truck. His right arm was around the willowy female, and he leaned toward her, intent on what she said. He quickly kissed her, and his head came back in a huge laugh.

"I'm a dunce!" I muttered. My face burned, turning red. "He has a girlfriend!" Flinching, I hurried to the entry before he could see me. Devastated, I felt numb with the realization I was falling for him.

Joel

It was done. Patricia was over. Thank God she found someone who wanted the same things she did. It wasn't me, that was for dang sure. It was a relief to hear her plans. I was free of her expectations that I would change and crawl back to her. She was a beauty, but under all that beauty was a spoiled child. I could never live up to her vision of a good husband. It wasn't in me to climb a company ladder. Been there, done that.

I tried. I had wanted to be that corporate bigshot. For about a minute. When I left the job, I felt free. Telling Patricia that I would manage the buildings until I had enough money to finance the sale was a disaster. She had lifted her chin and pouted. "I can't see us living in a dumpy apartment after we get married."

"Vintage apartment," I said.

"No," she insisted, "Dumpy,"

It went downhill from there.

But what the hell was Merry's ex doing there? He startled me, and I glimpsed her seeing him off. It was all I could do to give Patricia my blessings. Merry said she was done with this guy. Was she really?

Chapter 25

Merry

NOVEMBER 30

I breezed in with groceries and chow for Fido. A major storm was forecasted with multiple inches of snow. I parked the car in the 'safe' zone where it wouldn't be ticketed and towed during the snowstorm. After taking Fido out, I collected the mail. Among the bills and advertising, there was a notice requesting a signature for a letter at the post office. Sighing, I checked the time, and left Fido at home.

My nerves were on edge as I drove, hoping no one would take my parking spot. The car crawled the two miles through heavy snow to the post office. The lobby was empty, and I signed and handed the form to the clerk.

With trembling fingers, I opened the letter. It was a 30-day notice to vacate the premises. My stomach dropped. I scanned the form letter. Cursing, I started for home. The notice stated the building would no longer have dogs. As a dog owner, if I did not remove the dog within 30 days, I was subject to eviction. I was furious. The

Goldmans may have just as well taken out my heart and stomped on it.

At home, I sank down on the sofa, Fido at my side, and called Aunt Liz. With a litany of grousing, I told her I was being evicted.

"No!" she said.

"Yes!" I read from the letter, wailing. "THIRTY DAYS to remove the dog."

"You and Fido can live with me," she said.

"That's not the point!" I raged. "My dog is family! It would be like telling someone that they don't want to rent to anyone with children. It's inhumane!"

"Not exactly. You can stay with me until you find another pet-friendly place," she said, adding, "It'll be fun."

Calming down, I said, "Thank you. But I'm going to fight this. It is cruel and unusual to evict anyone in December, in Minnesota, before the holidays, no less!"

"Hmm. Maybe you can appeal to the management. They might Grandfather Fido in. You signed a lease stating you have a pet. You haven't been a nuisance, have you?" Her lilting voice ended on a flat note. "Why are they doing this?"

Searching my memory, I reflected, "There was that instance of pet waste in the recycle bin." Gulping, I said, "I didn't look at the container." Adding, "It did not happen again. He barks," I admitted. "As far as I know, it isn't excessive. If I'm here, he's good. But if Tom Kat taunts him or there are other noises, he barks. Joel forgave the two violations because of the work I did in the building. I do not get it!" Exasperated, I said, "It's a month-to-month lease."

"It isn't possible to be there 24/7. If I were you, I would talk to Joel. See if there is anything he can do," she said.

"I will. First, I have to calm down." A flash of Joel and the woman he kissed in the lot came to mind, and I grimaced.

"Yes." She chuckled. "Approach him with a rational mind. You don't want to blast him."

There was a rap at the door. "I have to go. Someone is here."

Sure enough, Joel stood in the hall.

"Yes?" I answered, still unnerved by the letter.

"Hi, Merry," he said, smiling. "I wanted to check on you and remind you to park your car in the area that won't get ticketed and towed."

"Yeah. Right," I snarked. "I'm sure you're very concerned about your residents."

"Huh?" He frowned.

I waved the notice in his face. "The Goldmans are throwing me and Fido out in December. During the winter. Before the holidays! Have a great day!" I shut the door.

"Merry! I didn't know anything about this. Believe me. Open up," he begged.

Slowly, I opened the door. His face was ashen. "There must be some mistake. I'll talk to them."

"How could you *not* know?" I demanded. "You oversee the buildings and the residents!"

"I'm not sure what's going on." He frowned. "I'll find out."

"Do that!" I slammed the door.

So much for staying calm in the face of a storm. I cuddled with Fido in the living room, my mind a jumble of outrage and resignation. Where was I going to go? If the building owners didn't want a dog living in their building, I did not want to stay here. I didn't want to dump my problems on Aunt Liz. I had to handle them myself.

Still, it was winter. If I couldn't find another place to live, I would suck it up and go to Aunt Liz's. I would have to, for Fido's well-being. With that resolve, I looked through my storage closet for boxes I had kept from the move to Holly Street and started packing. I did not want to stay here, even if Joel resolved things with the Goldmans. I was hurt and felt like a fool. It was silly that I had found the building manager attractive, with his wavy brown hair, twinkling blue eyes, and deep dimples.

Chapter 26

Merry

OVER THE WEEKEND, THE streets were plowed, but another round of snow was forecasted for later that night. Taking advantage of the brief break in weather, I stacked the packed boxes in a corner of the living room and made a trip to the store to get more. Joel hadn't come back, and with each passing night, I felt it was probable that he didn't have any sway with the owners and was avoiding me. I knew I did not want to live in a building managed by TREM, but there were few vacancies this time of year. I resigned myself to staying with Aunt Liz. It was too much—a job search and now looking for a dog friendly place to live.

Numb, I fell into bed at night, too tired to talk, even to Aunt Liz.

Arf, arf! Fido nosed me awake and continued his insistent barking. I checked the time. Midnight.

"Hush. Fido!" I shushed the dog and tried to get back to slumber—a welcome space in my life.

Arf, arf! He became more animated with his barks coursing through his body. I shoved the covers aside and jumped out of bed. Slipping on my robe, I went to the kitchen, with Fido close on my heels. Cracking the door open, I peered out. Fido dashed into the hall, his barking excited and high-pitched. Running to catch him; he danced out of my reach, his body rigid with angst. He ran from door-to-door yapping, and then up to the third floor.

I dashed back to my apartment with Fido's barking echoing through the building. Overhead, I heard footfalls and the sound of a door splintering. I dialed 9-1-1, and yelled, "There's a break-in at Holly Street!" Grabbing a coat and Fido's leash, I hurried out. Other residents emerged from their homes and stood in the hall, rubbing sleep from their eyes.

"What's going on?" One woman demanded, a coat over her pajamas.

"I heard a door breaking. My dog keeps barking," I said, frantic to get Fido.

Fido dashed from the third floor to me, panting. Finally catching him, I heard sirens and went downstairs. Other residents and I milled around the front entry. Light snow was falling, and we stayed put, watching the street. I clung to Fido and stepped aside when the fire engine arrived, along with police and ambulance vehicles.

"Is anyone injured?" a policeman asked.

We looked at one another and shook our heads.

"I heard a commotion on the third floor. It sounded like a door breaking," I said. "I called 9-1-1."

"I thought there was a fire?" Another man countered.

"We need EMTs up here. There's a man down!" Joel yelled from the top of the third-floor staircase.

Paramedics entered behind a policeman with a gurney and hurried up the stairs, lugging equipment. It sounded like a stampede with heavy footfalls climbing the stairs to the top floor of the building. The residents lingered along the first-floor hallway, and looked at each other, uncertain. We craned our necks, trying to decipher what was happening. Shortly, the paramedics brought down a middle-aged man on a stretcher, who I recognized from a casual nod, and who lived in a third-floor apartment. Everyone stood back to let the EMTs through. The firefighters and police followed the EMTs out. Joel was last, and he said, "It's okay. Everyone can go back to their homes. I broke into Mr. Baker's apartment to get to him."

"Folks, we checked out the building. It appears that Mr. Baker lit a candle and fell asleep. The candle tipped over into his armchair and smoldered," a policeman said. The firefighter standing next to him nodded. "There is no fire."

"Why weren't the alarms working?" a resident demanded. "I heard the dog barking."

"That was Fido," I said. "He must have smelled smoke from Mr. Baker's apartment."

"What about the alarms?" another woman yelled.

"I'll inspect the fire alarms tonight. Now, everyone, please go back to your homes and try to get more sleep," Joel said.

It was three o'clock in the morning, and we trudged back to our homes. On the walk back, I heard residents murmuring, "Thank goodness for the little mutt barking. It could have been bad." I smiled and hugged Fido a little closer and gave him an extra special treat of liverwurst before heading back to bed.

Too wound up to sleep, I showered and dressed for the day. On a whim, I went to the third-floor apartment to see what happened. The door was closed with yellow caution tape. The hinges were bent, and the frame was splintered. I sniffed the air. Lingering smoke. Joel's apartment was next to Mr. Baker's, and I hesitated, being so close to his place. As if he sensed my presence in the hall, he opened his door. I stopped and stared, startled. He stared back.

"Taking a tour of the damage?" he asked grimly.

"I was curious," I admitted.

"It was quite a night." He sighed. "Fido's barking woke me. I could tell something was wrong and banged on Mr. Baker's door, trying to rouse him. When he didn't answer, I forced the door and broke the frame. I didn't want to delay getting inside if he was hurt."

"Okay."

"There was a throw pillow smoldering on the chair next to the sofa. I picked it up and beat out the smoke by stomping it. I found a pot in the kitchen, filled it with water, doused the chair. It was good Fido woke me when he did."

"What happened to Mr. Baker?"

"I think he had a medical emergency and passed out. It looked as though he tried to get up and stumbled. A glass and a plate littered the floor. He was lying on the sofa and his breathing was heavy, but he wouldn't wake when I shook him."

"That's awful."

"Yes. It was terrible." He rubbed his face. Fatigue lined his forehead, and there were deep circles under his eyes. "When I spoke with the Goldmans, they said they would call his emergency contact. He has a daughter who lives close by."

"That's good."

"His apartment will need to be repainted."

"Uh, huh."

"I told the Goldmans about how the dog alerted the residents and woke me."

"Uh, huh."

"A cat doesn't bark," he said with a small smile.

"Nope, sure doesn't." I nodded.

"They are going to drop the 'no dogs' notice to tenants." He looked sheepish.

"Good!"

"I'm sorry there had to be an emergency for them to decide that," Joel said.

"You and me both," I said, not sure how I felt about staying now. "What happened with the alarms?"

"Someone tampered with them." He was short. "I am working with the fire inspector. The alarm system's breaker was tripped."

"Who would mess with fire alarms?" I frowned. "That's serious business."

"Yes."

"I can't believe it would have been Benjamin," I thought aloud. "Vandalizing a display is one thing, but turning off fire alarms could mean death."

"Yes. Believe me, I thought of that." Joel stroked his chin, exasperated. "The police are investigating. I gave them the video with Benjamin. That was before the cameras went out again."

"The cameras went out?"

"Someone damaged them a few days ago. I couldn't retrieve any new images, and the internet was down."

"So, whoever damaged the cameras this time may have tampered with the alarms at the same time?"

"Maybe. I put the surveillance cameras on the back burner to get ready for the storm. We won the contest. It didn't seem necessary to monitor the displays any longer."

He saw the look on my face, and hastily added, "Not that they aren't important. Other things happened that took priority."

"Like packing," I grumbled.

"What?" His brows furrowed; his eyes dimmed.

"You didn't expect me to get rid of Fido and still *live here*?" I was indignant.

"I said I would talk to the Goldmans." He was defensive.

"Yeah. Well, I haven't heard from you, and besides, talk is cheap!"

"I've been busy." He threw up his hands. "We've had a foot of—"

"I see!" I flushed bright red, and I bit my lip. "You've been *busy!*"

"What does that mean?" He frowned.

"Nothing." I muttered. "It is none of my business."

He stared for a moment, then realization flashed on his face. "You saw me with Patricia in the parking lot. I thought that was you running into the building."

"Maybe." My stomach tumbled. It had been Patricia, his ex, and even worse, he had seen me.

"Now we're even." He gave a small smile.

"What?" I frowned.

"I saw you outside with that geeky-looking guy. He followed you up to your apartment. Not that I was watching, mind you. It is part of my job to know who comes and goes in the building. Whether they are friend or foe."

"Okay. You go first," I said, tilting my head, placing my hands on my hips.

"Patricia wanted my blessing. She and her new man have set a wedding date, and she didn't want any bad feelings between us to jinx her new marriage. She even invited me to the wedding."

"Wow. And you gave her your blessing?" I recalled the quick kiss.

"I did. Holding on to a hurt like that damages you more than the person who did the hurting," he said soberly and gazed at me. "Okay, that was a mouthful. Now you."

"It was Derrick, my ex," I admitted.

"And?" His eyes lowered, and he waited.

"I let him down easy."

"He wants to get back together?"

"Yes." I nodded. "But I couldn't ever trust him again."

"It's hard to trust again." He nodded; his lips tight.

"It is," I agreed, "Aunt Liz said I had to forgive myself, too."

"Yes. Sometimes that's harder than forgiving the other person." His soft gaze warmed me.

I met his look with a smile; my head tilted. "You get it."

"Sure do." He was solemn.

"That was part of why I saw Derrick again. And,"—I laughed—"because he was acting like a freaking stalker standing outside my building."

"He didn't call?"

"No."

"That's creepy." He snorted. "At least Patricia called before she came."

"Oh, she did, did she?" I teased.

"Yes."

"Are you going to the wedding?" I asked.

"Good grief, no. Forgiveness, yes. Nothing more."

"You are, for sure, over her?" I blushed.

"I am." His tone was firm. "And you? How do you feel about Derrick?"

"We're done." I smiled. My shoulders felt lighter, and I was relieved and happier than I had been in a long while. Joel stepped toward me and wrapped his arms around me. Resting my head against his firm chest, I heard the thump of his heartbeat. He stroked my hair. "I'm glad," he whispered. Fido whined and gave a bark. Joel loosened his grip. "Maybe you should have a talk with Fido." He chuckled.

"Aww. Come on, group hug." I scooped him up. Joel grinned, and we stood together in a huddle. His hands fell away, and facing me, he asked, "Can you help get Mr. Baker's unit fixed up while he's in the hospital? I don't want him to come home to a mess."

"Sure."

"I will talk to his daughter about what he likes and let her know I'll replace whatever the smoke damaged. The chair and a few furnishings can go." Joel ran his hands through his hair. "I'll see when he's due to get out."

"Sounds good."

"How did it go with the fire inspection?"

"Okay. I locked the circuit breaker panel."

"Where is the panel?" I asked.

"It's in the basement, in the laundry room."

"Oh?" Tilting my head, recalling the room. "That's right, in the corner." I shook my head. "It's a shame people can't be trusted."

"It could have been kids playing around. This way, it will be more secure. Probably should have done that earlier."

"It's a pain to lock the panel. It's harder to access," I said.

"That's okay. I can work with it."

"So, if they didn't trip any of the other circuits, someone had to have picked the fire circuit to throw. Surely, they are marked," I mused.

"They are. We don't know." He lifted his shoulders. "I hope it isn't someone with a vendetta. Fires in an apartment are not typical. I don't know if it's ever happened here before."

"Yes. I suppose. Maybe someone was hoping for a random fire?" I asked, puzzled.

"I think it's a coincidence. Now that the panel is locked, no intruder can trip a circuit."

"That's good." I sighed. "We may never know."

"We don't know how long the circuit was off. This is a large building, with people coming and going. Friends and relatives visit. Not everyone is a resident."

Joel

I was relieved that Merry and I had it out about Patricia and Derrick. It's creepy that Derrick keeps hanging around. Thank goodness Patricia is off to her knight in shining armor, and I wouldn't have to worry about measuring up to a corporate tycoon. I dodged a bullet. I am not a suit kind of guy.

The group hug was special, with Merry's body close to mine, along with the dog's. Drat the little mutt. At least he's warming up to me.

I want to spend more time with Merry. Could she be the one? Her sweet smile was a balm. Beneath the smile, there is a passion waiting for the right man. Me.

It is time to ask her out on a real date.

Chapter 27

Merry

Mr. Baker's daughter gave us the go-ahead to toss anything that we couldn't salvage from the smokey smell. According to her, he wasn't picky about colors, but he liked the color blue, and clean lines—no flowers or gaudy colors.

"A man with simple tastes; after my heart," Joel joked when we discussed how to redo the apartment. "I have a recliner coming next week, and I've thrown the old beast of a chair out. It had to have been a relic from the '40s."

"But the horsehair fill was a good thing. It's naturally fire retardant," I said.

"It is. I checked the new furniture tags for fire retardancy." He smiled. "We're good."

I chose a blue color to keep the apartment light. Joel replaced aged window shades while I painted to the music of Motown on my CD player.

"It's kind of cute that you like those old songs," Joel commented, after he finished installing new window blinds. "They're classics."

"It reminds me of growing up with Aunt Liz. She had the Temptations, Dionne Warwick, Gladys Knight, or Martha Reeves and the Vandellas playing while we cleaned the house on Saturday mornings. Then we would go to the movies in the afternoon." I chuckled.

"Your Aunt Liz sounds like fun," he said.

"She is." I smiled.

The Temptations blared out My Girl, and Joel grinned, took the paintbrush from my hand, and drew me towards him, and we swayed to the tune. Together, we sang the words to the song. My face flushed. When the tune ended, I stepped away awkwardly. He bowed.

"Thank you for the dance."

Flipping my hair back, I murmured, "Thank you." I reached for the brush in the paint pan, trying to keep my cool, my stomach churning.

He cleared his throat, gave a sideways smile, and asked, "You were talking about your aunt?" He turned back to testing the blinds.

"Yes. Aunt Liz is fun." Recovering my composure, as I painted. "She didn't have an easy time after her husband died, but she tried to make everything better after losing my parents."

"How old were you when that happened?"

"Seven." I frowned. "I was in first grade. The principal and the counselor came to my classroom and told me there had been an accident. After that, I went to live with Aunt Liz and Uncle Al. It's all a blur." I shrugged.

"Uncle Al?"

"Yes. He died when I was ten. Cancer. Since then, it has been Aunt Liz and me."

"That's rough."

"You said your parents have passed, too. When was that?"

"I was a teenager, fourteen." His brows furrowed as he recounted, "They went out on New Year's Eve to celebrate and never came home. Their car was T-boned by a drunk driver."

"I'm sorry." I gasped, stopped painting, and stared at him.

"Yep. It was tough." He adjusted the window blind. "My aunt and uncle took me in, but I acted out. Did some stupid stuff that got me thrown in juvenile hall. That straightened me out." He glanced at me. "Now you know the story of my life." He shrugged.

"Uh, huh. I think there's more," I said. My eyes widened.

"That's enough for now," he said, short. "I brought the upholstery machine, and I'll start cleaning the sofa."

"So, that'll take care of the smoke smell?"

"I spread baking soda over the couch and vacuumed it earlier to absorb the odor. If it does not work after a cleaning, Mr. Baker will get a new sofa, too." He grinned.

"It is nice you're doing this for him."

"His daughter doesn't have a lot of time with a full-time job and a family. He has been a good tenant. I don't like to see anyone have a hard time of it. Especially this time of year."

"What happened to him?"

"His daughter said it was a heart attack. He is going to stay with her until he's okay to live on his own. She thinks he will be back around the first of the year. She is paying his rent in the meantime. And,"—he grimaced—"no more candles for Mr. Baker."

"You told her that?" I asked.

"She told me." He filled the water container for the cleaner. "It'll be noisy," he warned and plugged in the machine. I nodded and went back to painting. Out of the corner of my eyes, I watched his muscular arms move the machine over the couch. He brushed a lock of hair from his forehead while he worked. He caught my gaze and grinned. I flushed and turned back to the project at hand, hiding my embarrassment at being busted.

The door to the apartment was open while we worked. Suddenly, a streak of black fur dashed in and a paw swiped at Joel's leg as he ran the cleaner. He switched off the machine, laughing. "Tom Kat's hungry!"

"So funny." I giggled. Tom Kat sat on his haunches, his tail swishing back and forth.

"Duty calls," Joel said. "Good time to take a break." He viewed my progress in painting.

"I'll paint to the corner, then check on Fido and eat lunch." I brought the roller to the edge and finished the inside with a brush. We broke for lunch. Tom Kat rode Joel's shoulder to his apartment, while I went to mine.

After lunch, we worked companionably for the rest of the day. I finished painting, and Joel finished cleaning the upholstery and washed down the kitchen cabinetry along with any other surfaces that hinted of smoke.

We walked through the apartment at the end of the day.

"Looks good," Joel said approvingly. "The place smells better and placing containers of white vinegar will absorb any more smells."

"It's coming together." Pleased, I viewed the area.

"I'll walk you home," he said.

"That would be nice." Smiling, we ambled to my apartment. He stood inside by the kitchen table while I collected Fido. "You're spending Christmas with your aunt and uncle?"

"They don't celebrate Christmas," he said.

"Oh?"

"Hanukkah."

"Okay?"

"My father was Irish Catholic. My mother was Jewish." He added with a grin, "It could get noisy when the subject of religion came up."

"Would you like to come with me to my aunt's home for Christmas dinner?" I blurted. "She loves entertaining on the holidays."

"I'd like that." The door was ajar while we talked, and I had Fido leashed, ready to go out, when Tom Kat darted from the hall and climbed Joel's pant legs. He absently took him to his shoulder and held the cat while we talked. His body was at an angle to the kitchen counter. Fido whimpered and barked. The cat sprang from his shoulder onto the counter, and Fido went wild, barking and jumping. Tom Kat spied a milk bone on the counter and batted it to the floor. Fido went for the treat.

It all happened in a flash. Joel and I, startled, looked at each other and started laughing.

"I guess that's a truce," Joel said and grabbed Tom Kat. "I'll get this guy home." He stood at the door, hesitating. "Would you like to go with me to the reindeer and llama welcome event this weekend? They have food trucks, and people can pet the animals."

"That'd be fun!" I exclaimed. "It is at the riverfront park?"

"Yes. At noon on Saturday."

"Just the two of us, right? No Fido or Tom Kat? Fido is not very social. Is this a date?" I blurted, suddenly shy. I was used to working on projects with Joel. A light kiss here and there. A date, even in a crowd, seemed daunting. His eyes twinkled.

"If that makes you nervous, we don't have to call it a date. I'd like to spend time with you without work or pets. How about we say it isn't a date? Maybe we call it 'going out' or a 'meetup'."

"Isn't that the same thing?" My brows furrowed.

"Yes." He winked. "But we don't need to label it a date."

"Okay." I blushed furiously, happy at the prospect of spending time together, but still too nervous to say "date."

"In the meantime, I'll see you tomorrow." He leaned in for a quick kiss, and I melted at the softness of his lips. Closing the door, I grinned at Fido. "Looks like I'm going out, and Tom Kat likes you."

I fed Fido, showered, and grabbed a sandwich for dinner. Then called Aunt Liz. "I hope you don't mind; I asked Joel, the maintenance man, to Christmas dinner."

"Not at all. The more the merrier. I asked one of my pickleball players," she said.

"Pickleball?"

"Yes. It's all the rage. It's like ping-pong with a small paddle, only on a court, like tennis."

"Okay. What happened to knitting?"

"Too sedentary. I need to move."

"It sounds like excellent exercise," I agreed, trying to visualize Aunt Liz on a tennis court. My forehead creased at the vision.

"It is. You have been busy?" she asked.

"I've been helping Joel get the apartment cleaned up for Mr. Baker's return."

"It is a bummer about that fire. It scares me that the alarms weren't working. Especially in an older building, it could be a firetrap."

"The fire investigator is examining," I said. It worried me too, but I didn't need to burden Aunt Liz. "The good thing is that Joel said the Goldmans won't evict anyone with a dog. Fido earned his keep by barking and alerting the residents."

"Wonderful! When will the fire inspector's report be out?"

"Not sure."

"You are spending a fair amount of time with this Joel fellow," Aunt Liz said.

"It's work." I crossed my fingers. I wasn't ready to face my growing feelings for the handsome building manager with the easy smile, let alone talk to Aunt Liz about him. She hadn't found any more matches for me, and I hoped she'd forgotten about marrying me off.

"Ha!" she teased.

"Sort of," I admitted. "He is handsome."

"And handy. You know what that old comic, Red Green, said. 'If you ain't handsome, you gotta be handy.'"

"Oh, boy," I groaned.

"Joel is handsome and handy." She giggled. "Dinner is at two o'clock, as usual."

Joel

She said YES! Grinning, as I left Merry's apartment. I nearly bailed on asking her out, but she said YES! I booked it out before she changed her mind. Working with her tomorrow in Mr. Baker's apartment would be a challenge. She is a fox, a shy fox.

Asking me to Christmas dinner with her aunt was a bonus. I can't wait to spend time with her and her aunt. I have to keep my cool. Don't call this Saturday a date because that scared her. Scares me, too. Just take it slow and easy.

Chapter 28

Merry

At eleven-thirty Saturday morning, Joel arrived at my door, freshly shaved, smelling heavenly, and wearing a hooded jean jacket, a new plaid flannel shirt, and blue jeans.

"You're sure this isn't a date?" I asked. "Because I'm not into dating right now." Overnight, the possibility of an actual date with Joel had brought on anxiety, complete with a nervous stomach and eye tic.

"We won't call it a date," he said. His dimples deepened, his lashes long. "If you don't want to."

"Yeah. Okay, not a date." I was still befuddled. I pressed my eye to keep it still. It had been all I could do to behave normally. Well, sort of normal. While we worked on Mr. Baker's apartment the day earlier, I had thrown myself into the final stages of finishing the apartment. Joel had been jovial while he worked at changing out a fixture that we had decided needed an update. He had not appeared flustered at all. Curse that even temperament.

Despite my angst, I had pulled myself together for the non-date, wearing suitable attire of a black hooded jacket, black and white scarf, red high-necked sweater, and blue jeans. A glance in the mirror said I looked good. Fido had followed and watched my every move, as if he knew something was up.

He had leaped to attention at Joel's knock, and I held him back. Tentatively, Joel held out his hand for the dog to sniff. He brought out a treat from his pocket and offered it. Fido snatched it up, and I put him down; he ran off with his goodie. You found the key to Fido's heart," I said, smiling.

"I did, with Tom Kat's help!" He chuckled. We laughed, remembering the cat's antics. He grew serious then, and said, "I have a confession."

My stomach lurched. Was he backing out of our non-date?

He cleared his throat.

"When I was a kid, a dog bit me."

"Oh no. I am sorry! What happened?"

"I was a first-grader waiting for the bus, and the neighbor's dog escaped out of their front door. I tried to catch him, rushed at the animal, and got to it before the owner. The dog bit me and ran off."

"I am sorry. Were you hurt?" I winced.

"Just a bruised ego. The kids on the bus thought it was funny. I fell and dropped my pack. The neighbor checked my hand and ran off. He didn't even say he was sorry."

"So, you have an attitude about dog owners?" I was defensive. "Pets are like family. It's kind of like a toddler who might shriek at a person who surprised them."

"I know. I feel the same about Tom Kat." He relaxed. "But since then, I've been wary of little terriers, like this one here." Fido was happily munching in the living room.

"I am very cautious with Fido around anyone. He is fast and fierce." I nodded. "You've learned how to approach him." I shrugged. "He seems okay with you."

"Yes. I have mastered the art of taming the dog," he joked. "I wanted you to know, that's all."

"Thank you. That means a lot to me." Joel's confession about why he didn't like dogs warmed my heart. He trusted me with his secret.

He led the way to his truck, which was warming up for our drive to the meet and greet of the festival's traditional reindeer and this year's extra attraction, llamas.

***

People lined the streets, waiting for the grand arrival of Santa in his sleigh. Santa called out a huge 'Ho ho ho,' while the sleigh carried Mr. and Mrs. Claus to the riverfront area. Parking the sleigh in a cordoned off area, the pair dismounted and went to sit in thrones where elves awaited to take the children to meet Santa. More elves led the reindeer to a pen next to the llamas, and we weaved our way through the lineup of patrons eagerly waiting to pet the animals.

"They are awesome," I said, admiring the long, arched necks and fur of the llamas.

"Careful, if you get too close, they'll spit at you." He smiled, observing the graceful creatures.

Just then, a white llama reared its head and let out a stream of spit at a tall man who had leaned over the fence, startling the animal.

"See?" Joel grinned.

"Not so different from any other species." I chuckled. We continued to gaze, absorbed with the beauty of the animals and holiday decorations.

"How about some hot chocolate?" he asked, pointing. "There's a truck that sells hot cider, coffee, hot chocolate."

"Hot chocolate would be perfect, please."

"Wait here while I get it. Marshmallows or whipped cream?"

"Ooh, whipped cream, if they have it. Thank you." I nodded and watched his handsome profile as he weaved through the throngs of people to stand in line at the truck. He looked back at me, and gave a shrug, as if to say it would be a while. Relaxing, I leaned against a tree, watching the activity of the crowd with the children.

My back stiffened when I saw a man with a beaked nose and chunky eyeglass frames. He reached over to pet a llama and was treated with a stream of spit. Backing away and stumbling, he wiped the spit from his jacket. He looked up from where he dabbed at his coat and started. Our gazes locked. He sent me a slow, sly grin as recognition dawned. It was Benjamin. My stomach churned.

"Here you are." Joel offered a drink. "What's up?" His eyes searched my expression.

"Over there." I gestured. "That's Benjamin," I muttered, taking the hot chocolate smothered with whipped topping.

"Yep." He nodded, taking a long look. "That's the guy in the photo."

"What should we do?" I asked.

"Nothing." He shrugged. "We won the festival prize money. Vandalism is a property crime. It was not a high dollar loss, just a bump in the road to victory for us." He smiled, the corners of his blue eyes crinkled, caressing mine. "He will get his. Let's enjoy our non-date."

Relaxing, my stomach melted under his soft gaze, and I lifted my head, and his lips met mine.

"This is the best not-a-date ever," I said under my breath.

"Yep." Joel grinned. We straightened, avoiding the gazes of people around us. Self-conscious, I gulped the hot chocolate.

"Oh, my, this is good!" I glanced toward where Benjamin had stood and saw he had vanished. "Good riddance."

"Uh huh." Joel winked. "Let's see the tents," he said, gesturing with his drink. "Or get lunch at the turkey drumstick truck." His face creased with a wide grin. "We can't forget the dessert truck."

"You had me at desserts." I grinned. "Even after the yummy hot chocolate."

"Let's go." He grabbed my hand, and we spent the next three hours meandering through tents filled with homemade holiday ornaments, wreaths, and tchotchkes, admiring people's creativity. Between visiting tents, we bought frosted cookies, fudge, and anything that captured our attention. I admired Joel's instant camaraderie with the shopkeepers and townspeople. He squeezed my hand while we walked, only releasing it when food came into play.

"Have we seen it all?" he asked, gazing down at me with an easy smile, his hand resting on my shoulder. We stood outside the last tent filled with people.

"Are you sure we ate everything?" I groaned. I had declined most items, with Joel offering to share his food.

Even with a bite here and there, I was sure it surpassed the recommended daily calorie count for most adults.

"I think we did," he said. "Santa's leaving." We waved at Mr. and Mrs. Claus, and Santa let out another "Ho ho ho," and they bowed their heads to the crowd.

"We should go then." With a last look at the llamas in the pen, and the reindeer now gone with Santa, we headed back to his truck, hand in hand. My mind wandered, and I sneaked a peek at him as we strolled. *I am hooked, totally a goner in like with this guy.*

Joel

I wanted to go over to that Benjamin creep and punch him out or give him a piece of my mind. But it wasn't the right time or place. Merry was freaked enough about going on our non-date. I didn't want to turn it into a face-off with the jerk.

Her face lit up like an angel when she petted the llama and reindeer. The joy she had walking through the holiday festival was exhilarating, and it was all I could do to keep my hands off her. My bad.

How could I tell her about my agreement with the Goldmans? The festival money was my chance to lock down the payment for taking over the buildings. It was my guilty pleasure working with Merry. She was sensitive about not disclosing about her ex with good cause. He was a piece of work. It would be a struggle to keep my cool while we worked on the apartments, but, what a challenge.

Chapter 29

Merry

"I have news!" Kris called the next day, her voice bubbly. "TREM fired Benjamin!"

"When, why?" I asked. Okay, I felt a teensy bit of satisfaction at the news, after seeing him at the downtown festival.

"Mr. Bigg told me last night." She paused; her voice was reflective. "I saw Benjamin leave Mr. Bigg's office, looking upset about two weeks ago. Mr. Bigg said it was because Benjamin had gotten the heave ho." She gave a full-throated giggle.

Something in her voice made me ask, "Are you and Mr. Bigg seeing each other?"

"Maybe." She chortled, coy. "Anyway, I thought you would want to know. Mr. Bigg said one reason TREM fired Benjamin was because he promised he would win the Reindeer Festival decorating challenge, and he didn't. They thought he might juggle the books again."

"Really?" I asked, and added, "That would do it."

"Everyone saw you and your good friend on the news." Another giggle.

I thought quickly and looked at the calendar. "So, they fired him two weeks ago, on a Friday?"

"Yes. That is correct," she said.

"That same weekend, there was a fire here at the building."

"No way!"

"Yes. And the security cameras were bashed in again."

"What?" she gasped.

"The night before the festival judging on Black Friday, someone vandalized the displays and damaged the cameras. It was a major ordeal, getting the displays up in time for judging. After that, someone took out the cameras again, and we think, tampered with the fire alarms at the same time."

"OMG! Benjamin?"

"He might have." I was grim. "If he was angry enough, he could have snuck in and done something to the alarms. It was his face on video before the cameras went dark."

"No!"

"Yes."

"He always had this kind of sly look about him, like he had inside knowledge that no one else had," Kris said in a rush. "That creep!"

"Well, we don't know for sure. But it makes sense."

"Where was the fire?" she asked.

"In Mr. Baker's unit on the third floor."

"What happened?"

"His daughter said he had a heart attack. He must have stumbled and tipped a candle into a chair. His unit was the only one damaged, but the alarms didn't go off. Fido saved the day. He smelled the smoke and alerted the residents. The owners stopped the 'no dogs' plan because of Fido's barking. I was ready to move!"

"That is wonderful! They decided dogs *do* rule!" She laughed. "So, it was an accident in Mr. Baker's apartment?"

"Yes."

"The person who tampered with the alarm couldn't know anything would happen?"

"True. Mr. Baker lived alone. No visitors that I know of."

"A fire could have happened at any time?"

"Yes."

"Well." She sighed. "It is good that you didn't have any damage, and that you and Fido can stay put. You have enough going on with finding another job. How is that going?"

"I've been busy helping Joel get Mr. Baker's apartment repaired and put the job search on the back burner. With the winnings from the festival, I'm okay for now. I will pound the pavement hard after the new year."

"Sounds like a plan."

"So, what's going on with Mr. Bigg?"

"Oops. I have to go. We'll talk later." She giggled and hung up.

***

Joel and I made a last walk-through of Mr. Baker's apartment by checking all the rooms, lights, and appliances.

"It looks good. Excellent!" I said, happy with the results of our hard work.

"Yep. He can move back anytime."

"He's still at his daughter's?"

"Yes. She is getting his clothes cleaned and getting new bedding. They are planning the move for the new year. It seems fitting, new year, new start."

"He should love this."

"I think he will," he said, viewing the soft blue wall paint, new blue throw, and pillows. "Thank you for all your work."

"It was a pleasure," I said. "After the first, it's back to the job hunt for me."

"Maybe the new year will bring something better." He smiled.

"It would be nice." It did not thrill me going back to an office, staring at a computer. I loved being out and moving, seeing results of a creative redo.

"You're still coming to Christmas dinner at Aunt Liz's?" I asked.

"Wouldn't miss it." He grinned.

"She usually invites other people to dinner. She said she invited someone from her pickleball group this year."

"Pickleball?"

"It's a thing now," I said. "It's kind of like ping-pong only on a court." I shook my head. "You have to see it." Then an alarm sounded in my mind. *What if she is still trying to set me up?*

"Is something wrong?" Joel asked. His forehead creased, watching me.

"No. But I had better go. I want to check in with Aunt Liz about dinner." And hoped my face didn't look too stricken at the possibility Aunt Liz may have another potential match.

"I will stay here and wait for Mr. Baker's daughter. She should be here soon."

"We'll talk later." I gave Joel a quick hug and a bright smile. He held me close, and whispered, "Later, then." Breaking our warm embrace reluctantly, I left for my apartment and called Aunt Liz.

"I wanted to touch base about dinner plans for Christmas," I said.

"Two o'clock. Bring the dinner rolls and a dessert. There should be plenty, but I always worry there won't be enough food."

"Sure. You remember I invited Joel, too."

"Yes."

"You said you had someone new coming? From your pickleball group?"

"Yes. He is coming, too." Her voice faded, and she sounded vague.

"He?" A red flag went up. My shoulders stiffened.

"I must go, Merry. There is another call coming through that I have been waiting for. I'll see you and Joel on Christmas Day." She disconnected.

"Okay, then." I said to the receiver. I hung up, confused. Aunt Liz sounded frazzled. It wasn't like her. I guess I had to be satisfied that she said 'you and Joel' like we were together. Although I had said nothing, she had speculated about the handsome handyman, as she called him. She wouldn't dare try to fix me up if there was someone else in the picture. Would she?

My phone rang again. I frowned at the number: Kris. So soon?

"Do you have your television on?" Kris asked, frantic, excited.

"No."

"Quick, Channel 5 is covering a protest on Ivy Lane!" She hung up.

I hit the remote to the television in the living room. The local channel was interviewing a group marching outside of the building managed by TREM. The couple I had met earlier plodded through snow in front of the building with signs that said 'TREM violates tenant rights! No services, no rent!' Others chanted as they walked with more signs of protest, "We want garbage removed! Sidewalks cleared for safety's sake!" One middle-aged woman held a sign said, 'Exterminate TREM!'

The television reporter queried a woman carrying a child, "What is your story here?"

"Living conditions keep getting worse under TREM's management. We want the garbage removed, the sidewalk shoveled, and the mice and bugs exterminated. This used to be a good place to live!"

The reporter said to the camera, "You heard it here first. Reindeer residents are fed up with the new management on Ivy Lane!" And the station went to a break.

"Oh boy," I muttered. Fido barked, startled by the knock at the door. Joel stood in the hall, and I waved him in. "Did you see the news?"

"No." He frowned, puzzled. He followed me to the living room, and I switched channels, searching for any news coverage at Ivy Lane. Another channel was giving local news updates, and we caught the tail end of the protest coverage. "Big news in Reindeer Falls. A local landlord may lose his license to rent his property because garbage dumpsters are overflowing, along with several code violations. We love Reindeer Falls for its small-town atmosphere with pleasant living conditions," the news anchor said. "Angry tenants plan more protests over the holidays."

The marchers shouted when they saw a stocky, dark-haired, bushy-bearded man drive up in a black SUV and park. "There he is! That's the owner!" one woman yelled. "When are you going to exterminate and get rid of the garbage?"

"And shovel!" another protester blared.

"Soon," the man said. "Take responsibility for your units. If you don't take out your garbage, you get vermin. It is not my problem." A cigar dangled from one side of his mouth while he waved a pudgy hand.

"We take out our garbage. You don't pay the garbage haulers! I called them!" another woman yelled. "You haven't paid the bill! You got our rent, but you didn't pay them!"

"It is a misunderstanding. The check got lost in the mail," the owner declared.

"For over a month!" another man countered. "Our last pickup was Halloween!"

The news clip ended as police came and dispersed the crowd. I turned to Joel. He was angry.

"That protest is too close to our building on Ivy Lane. Any applicants wanting to live in our building are going to be turned off by the conditions of the building managed by TREM. Not to mention driving past tenant protests."

"Is there anything we can do?" I asked.

"The city must get rid of the landlord. Let's hope they do when they see the protests. This is a great town. It is terrible that it has come to this."

Chapter 30

Merry

"Derrick?" When I returned from taking Fido out, he appeared in the hallway with a forlorn look. "What are you doing here?" I asked, startled.

I scanned his appearance. Usually neat and well-groomed, his hair was shaggy and unkempt. His coat hung on his thin frame. His eyes were glassy.

"I miss you, Merry. Can I come in?"

"How did you get into the building?" I asked, hesitantly.

"Another resident held the door for me," he said. "Please."

It was Minnesota Nice to hold the door for another person entering behind them. The person likely hadn't looked. It was an automatic response. So much for the security system.

"Just for a moment. I have to make some calls," I said and stepped aside. I was back on the job hunt, trying to get more nibbles on my resume.

"This won't take long. Unless you want it to." He smiled. His grin wavered when he saw my reluctance.

Derrick entered and reached into his jacket pocket. I stood back, puzzled. He brought out a small red jewelry box.

"I have been thinking about us, Merry. A lot. I love you and want you back." He offered the box. I stiffened.

"Derrick, I don't feel the same way. We have talked about this."

"Take the ring, Merry. Please. I want you to have it even if you don't want me anymore. It is your wedding ring. I was a fool. I am sorry." He hung his head.

"No. Derrick, you need help. I don't want the ring. Have you been taking drugs? Your eyes are glassy, and you seem funny. Woozy or something?" My gaze narrowed.

"I don't sleep well," he confessed. "Caffeine doesn't wake me. Sleeping pills don't put me to sleep."

"How did you get here?"

"Uber."

I relaxed. At least he wasn't driving.

"Call them and go home. Get some sleep."

"Okay." He hung his head and stuffed the box back into his coat. "I'll go."

I opened the door and waited in the hall, watching him retreat. He took out his cell phone and dialed. Stepping back inside, I held Fido close. "That wore me out. I am sorry you had to see that." He licked my cheek with a worried look.

When had Derrick ever been so crazy? I tracked through the memories of our time together, and I couldn't think of any time he had been this distraught. We had been busy. He was in graduate school. I was working, going to school, making a home for us. There was a lump in the pit of my stomach. I hoped it was the last I would see of Derrick.

***

I talked to Aunt Liz later.

"The holidays can be hard for people. Some people don't have relatives or a special relationship. Some people don't like the relationships or relatives they have," Aunt Liz commiserated. "I'm sorry Derrick is having a hard time."

"Me, too."

"He has four sisters," she said. "Surely, one of them could talk to him."

"You would think," I said, puzzled, reflecting, then asked, "So, what kind of dessert or rolls should I bring for dinner?"

"Whatever you want." She paused. "Do you still keep in touch with Kris?"

"Okay," I said, thinking of desserts. "Yes, I do."

"Maybe you want to invite her if she hasn't any plans."

"I can do that."

In the back of my mind, I thought, *Aha, at least Aunt Liz could fix up the pickleball fellow with someone. She knows I am not interested.*

"Let me know."

"Sure."

"If she wants, she can bring a date."

"Okay." I was confused. Kris could bring a date. *Guess I must be paranoid.* I laughed. Aunt Liz would invite any strays she could. That was just her.

When I called Kris, she was exuberant.

"Yes! That would be wonderful. With everyone in different states, getting on a plane or driving this time of year makes for a difficult holiday. Travel is expensive and exhausting. It is much better if we have our holidays in the summer. The family is going to celebrate in July next year." Kris had a brother and nieces in Michigan. They had decided years ago that celebrating safely took precedent over the actual day. Often, she would go to a holiday movie to mark the occasion and celebrate later in the year with family.

"What can I bring for dinner?" Kris asked.

"Nothing. We will have plenty of food," I said. "Aunt Liz will be happy to see you. I will let her know. She said to bring a date if you would like."

"Even better. I may ask someone."

"Cool. Anyone I know?"

"Oops, gotta go. Thank you so much. Talk later," she said in a rush and clicked off.

I heard the dial tone and hung up, frowning. *Not again.*

Chapter 31

Merry

LATER THAT DAY, THE fire inspector knocked on my door and started grilling me about the fire. "So, you were here the night of the fire in Mr. Baker's apartment?"

"Yes."

"And your dog alerted the residents?"

"Yes. He smelled smoke. I didn't."

"Hmm. And the building owners had given you a notice to vacate because of your pet?" I squirmed and folded my arms across my chest.

"The notice said I had to get rid of my dog," I said evenly. I had let him in after a peek at his credentials. That probably hadn't set a friendly tone. But I did not like how this conversation was proceeding.

"Were you going to get rid of your dog?"

"No. I was going to move. I had started packing."

"But there was the fire, and suddenly your dog was the hero." He stared at Fido, whom I held in my arms, secure from lunging at the man.

"Fido alerted the building residents by barking when the alarm didn't go off," I replied, my teeth gritted. "Where are you going with this?" My face felt hot as I studied the inspector.

"I am investigating all the possibilities. You benefited from the fire."

"What do you mean?" I frowned.

"The owners kept you and your dog as tenants. You didn't have to get rid of the dog. In addition, I was told that Joel, the building manager, employed you to redo the apartment. You are a designer?" He looked over notes on a notepad.

"You could say that. I am between jobs, and he has been kind enough to employ me while I look for work."

"What is your usual occupation?"

"Data entry," I said flatly.

"But you want to design." He looked up from his notes and smiled with raised brows.

"It's a passion, and I hope to make the change." My stomach dipped.

"There are a couple of lucky coincidences for you in the building fire."

"What are you getting at?" I was angry.

"Nothing, Ms. Ernst. Just asking questions. Your name and your dog come up frequently with other tenants." He coolly locked eyes with mine.

"If there is nothing else, Inspector, I want to get back to my job search." I held Fido under one arm, a warning rumble in his throat, and held the door open.

"Finished. For now." He sent me a tight grimace and left.

Shutting the door, I whispered, "Thank you for growling, Fido. But you didn't do me any favors with that guy."

***

An hour later, Joel rapped on my door. He smiled as I let him in, and his blue eyes twinkled. "Was that Derrick I saw in the hall earlier today?"

"Yes." My shoulders stiffened, and I went to the living room and sat on the sofa in front of my computer on the coffee table.

"It didn't go well," he said, scanning my face.

"No." I said dully. I glanced at him, and he looked sympathetic as he lowered his body into the easy chair next to the sofa.

"You don't want to talk about it?" he asked.

"No." I was short. Still upset about the fire inspector inquisition, I confronted him, "Do the residents think I messed with the circuit breaker?"

"No!" he said. "Who on earth told you that?"

"The fire inspector hinted at that," I said flatly.

"What do you mean?" he asked, puzzled.

"He was here. He knew I had received notice that Fido had to go. Because he alerted the residents the night of Mr. Baker's fire, it benefitted me, because the owners changed their mind about Fido."

"OMG." Joel erupted. "That is just plain crazy! No one has a beef with Fido. They're happy he is here."

"Then why did the owners want to evict him?"

"They thought it was better to have the same pet policy at each building, here and at Ivy Lane."

"That's it?" I stared at him, skeptical.

"They heard a dog barking occasionally, and they found pet waste in the parking lot." Shrugging, he leaned over and examined his hands.

"He is a dog. Dogs bark. There was one time, when it snowed, I didn't get to his waste," I conceded. "Joel, I think it's best I move. I do not see any way I can stay here with the suspicion I had anything to do with the alarms. Not to mention the fire inspector."

"I don't want you to go." He got up and sat next to me on the sofa, his fingers softly stroked my knee.

I leaped up and said, "Please go, Joel! Whatever this is, it is not working! Let's just stop!"

Hurt flashed across his face, and he slowly rose and walked out.

***

"It only makes you look guilty if you move, Merry," Aunt Liz said. "Do you like the apartment?"

"Yes."

"Does Fido like the apartment?"

"Yes."

"Then, stand your ground."

"It's too late. I gave them my notice," I said. After Joel left, I had called the Goldmans and gave them verbal notice, with a promise to send a letter, which I did that night. "I don't want to be suspected of being a firebug."

"You're mad about the inspector."

"Wouldn't you be?" I was exasperated. "Whose side are you on?"

"Yours," she replied firmly.

"Okay, sorry," I muttered. "It's been stressful."

"I know," she said. "So, when do you have to be out?"

"February 1. It was too late to give notice for the first of the year."

"Okay. Well, it is cutting it close. This time of year, is difficult to look for another place. You can stay with me," she said.

"Thanks, Aunt Liz. I will start looking for another apartment and step up my job search. What's a little more stress?"

"Merry. Stay with me. Until you get on your feet." She was firm.

"Thank you, but I don't want to lay my problems on you," I countered.

"We all need help sometimes. But I understand you want to resolve this yourself. I respect that. It is only if nothing else clicks. Pet-friendly is hard to find."

"Don't I know it," I grumbled, and changed the subject. "Hey, how about carrot cake bars with cream cheese frosting for the holiday dinner? It is a little different from our usual pie. Croissants for dinner rolls? Change is good?"

"I love carrot cake! Croissants would be lovely." Aunt Liz agreed. "I can't believe it is coming so quickly. The holiday is next Sunday! I must get busy if I am having guests for dinner."

"Is there anything else I can do?"

"Goodness. You have enough to do. You are still bringing Joel?"

"No. I think he understands he is uninvited."

"Harsh," she commented.

"Yes. But he wasn't exactly in my corner about my dog. And Fido and I are a team."

"Uh, huh."

"I should go. I will see you on Sunday. Call me if there is anything at all I can do," I said.

"Will do."

Joel

I didn't know the inspector would jump Merry about the fire. She had nothing to do with it. Her little mutt saved the day. It cut like a knife that she wants to move and quit whatever we were. I was about to spill the news about taking over the buildings, and I couldn't. I was mute. She was so blasted stubborn, and I couldn't speak in the face of her pig-headedness. I have to convince her to stay; I cannot bear to lose the woman I've fallen in love with because of a stupid misunderstanding.

Chapter 32

Merry

I SPENT THE REST of the week hunched over my computer, searching out jobs and places to live. It was becoming clear that if I didn't have a job, landlords were not interested.

"Another fine mess," I muttered. Taking a break on Friday, I started the bars for Aunt Liz's party and went out for the croissants that afternoon. I left the bars cooling on the stove while I headed out.

Laundry was also on the to do list. When I returned from the store, I took Fido out and got a load together and trekked down to the basement laundry machines.

Later, after taking a basket of clean clothes from the dryer, I pivoted and ran smack into Derrick.

"What are you doing here?" I gasped.

"Looking for you," he said. "Sorry, didn't mean to scare you."

Scrambling to pick up the spilled clothes while Derrick tossed a towel in the basket, I faced him. "I've got it," I fumed, and snapped, "Why?"

He held up his hands and backed up. "I wanted to wish you a wonderful holiday. You are busy. I'll go." His shoulders slumped, he walked away.

"Derrick, you need to call first!"

"Would you have seen me?" he retorted. He held up a hand in a wave and kept walking. I headed upstairs and inside my apartment.

"Good grief!" With a burst of energy, I folded the towels and washcloths. Then I slapped the side of my head. "Forgot the laundry soap. I will be back," and nodded towards Fido, who had found a warm towel to snuggle into.

I left the apartment unlocked while I dashed two flights down to the basement laundry. Snatching up the box of soap, my gaze went to the circuit breaker box, and I stopped. The new front that locked the box was broken. I inhaled, and my thoughts went in all directions. *Do I call Joel? If I call him, will he believe I hadn't done anything? Did Derrick tamper with the box? Do I tell Joel about Derrick? Should I check the breakers? No. Do not touch anything.* Backing out slowly, I was resigned. I had to report it to Joel. Whatever he thought, he thought. But, it was going to be awkward after I had told him to leave, to quit whatever we were. Grimly, I dialed him on my cellphone and reported the vandalism.

"I'll be right there," he said. Ten minutes later, he rapped on my door. "Tell me what happened." He looked weary and pensive. And very handsome with a scent of woodsy aftershave. But he didn't smile, and my shoulders felt heavy.

"Long story short, I was doing laundry. Derrick showed up and surprised me. He left. I had forgotten the soap, and I went back, then saw that the circuit box had been vandalized."

"Whoa. Derrick showed up? In the laundry room?"

"Yes."

"How'd he get in?" He frowned as he thought. "Someone let him in, Minnesota Nice strikes, again." He sighed. "Why was he here?"

"He said he wanted to wish me a happy holiday."

"He didn't call?" he asked.

"No, he didn't call." I was puzzled. "Yeah, why would he go to the basement laundry?"

Joel searched my face. "Unless he was the one who broke into the circuit box."

"But why?" I asked. I shook my head. Secretly, I had considered the same. But between the time I called Joel and when he came, I had dismissed the idea. Vandalism had not been Derrick's way of doing things.

"I'll repair the box first and then check the front entry camera video. It is fixed now, and we'll see if there is anything there."

"Okay." I was relieved that he didn't think I was responsible for the damage.

"I'll be back," he said. "Lock your door."

"Will do." Guiltily, I remembered I had left the door unlocked while I went back down to the laundry. Then I saw Fido. He had stirred when Joel knocked. After a few barks, he went back to the warm towel. He wouldn't let anyone in.

"Joel." I put my hand on his arm. He smiled for the first time, the weary look dissipated. "I'm sorry."

"Me, too." He stepped toward me, wrapped his muscular arms around me, and held me.

"I missed you," I said and rested my head against his firm chest. We stood together until Fido came over to investigate, sniffing our legs. Joel leaned toward me for a long kiss, and we lingered in our embrace until Fido barked. Laughing, we parted. I looked over at the pan of bars.

"I have to frost the dessert for Sunday."

"Yum." His eyes lit up, and he went to investigate the dessert. "What kind?"

"Carrot cake bars." I brought out the frosting I'd mixed and stowed in the fridge.

"I'll bet this is cream cheese frosting." He grinned at the bowl. "I could help?" he asked, hopefully. "Lick the spatula?"

"Sure." I laughed.

"I'll fix the breaker box and come back." He left with a quick kiss on my forehead.

I frosted the bars, covered them with plastic wrap, stashed them in the fridge, and puttered in the kitchen until Joel returned, helping himself to the spatula and bowl. I leaned back against the counter, enjoying his presence while he made quick work of the icing.

"So, the box wasn't too badly damaged?" I asked.

"Whoever did it, knew how to take it apart. It takes a screwdriver to loosen the face," he said. "I replaced the screws and tightened it up."

"Then someone came prepared with a screwdriver?" I asked, squirming.

"Looks that way to me." He was short. Finished with the bowl, he took it to the sink.

"I'll get that." I took the bowl and washed it.

"Delicious!" He smacked his lips. "How about we order dinner and go through the video for the camera?"

"Great idea."

That evening, after we ate Chinese food, we hunkered on the sofa while Joel scrolled through the video footage of the building's entrance.

"There's Derrick," I said, pointing at the thin figure. "And there he is, leaving."

"Uh, huh. Looks like he's been hit from the way his shoulders slump," Joel said.

"I was firm," I said. "I told him I wanted to be friends, nothing more. He wasn't listening."

His eyes held laughter, and he said, "Been there."

"Yeah. Okay, well, I am not fond of being considered a possible vandal."

"You are not a vandal," he said firmly. "The Goldmans said you gave notice that you were moving."

"Yes."

"You could change your mind?" He winked.

"No."

"Have you lined up a new place?"

"No, but I will. If not, Aunt Liz will let us stay with her. It will all work out." My jaw was tight, and I gave a quick nod.

"Sure." His eyes softened, and he went back to the video. "That's all there is. I didn't see anyone else who might be suspicious. Derrick wanted to wish you a wonderful holiday. We can't tell if he tampered with the box."

"Is there any way someone could come in the back entrance from the parking lot?" I asked. "Is there a camera?"

"No camera. Not unless they had a key." The back door didn't have a buzzer system like the front door. "Okay, I take that back. If someone held the door, like through the front entrance."

"Hmm."

"Are you coming on Sunday?" I asked.

"I have another invitation." He searched my face, a twinkle in his eyes.

"Of course." I couldn't expect him to drop plans he'd made after our fight. Flustered by his rejection and expression, I nodded. "Have a great holiday."

"Thank you," he said. "And you as well." He left with a warm hug and a soft kiss. I closed the door after him, trying to ignore the dull ache in my gut.

Chapter 33

Merry

Kris called early Saturday. "Did you see the morning news?"

"No." I flipped on the television. "OMG."

Reporters from local television stations were interviewing residents in front of the TREM-managed building on Ivy Lane. While I watched, with the phone to my ear, a group of people from City Hall addressed the crowd. A man identified himself as the mayor and spoke.

"The rental license of the owner of this building has been terminated," the mayor announced. "A new owner has purchased the property, and they will, along with the city, make the needed repairs and negotiate new leases. No one will be forced to move while this process takes place."

A roar went up from the crowd. The young couple I had met while touring the entry took the TREM sign down and ripped it to shreds. Another cheer went out.

"As I said, the city will help with the repairs. We have waste management coming to empty the dumpsters today." As he spoke, a yellow garbage truck drove in and noisily emptied the dumpsters. The mayor yelled over the turmoil, "And pest control is coming today to fumigate!"

Another cheer.

"This happens when people come together to make their voices heard in a peaceful and productive manner. The nonviolent protests and the signed petition from residents made for a speedy resolution. We look forward to a building residents can be proud of. We want the town of Reindeer to be the first choice for renters and homeowners alike! Happy holidays, everyone!" Another roar went out from the crowd and the newscast ended with a shot of a pest control van. I gasped and started.

Driving the vehicle was a man with a familiar broad nose and chunky black glasses. With a sly grin, he looked out at the crowd.

"It's Benjamin!" I stared at the television.

"Yes! That's him!" Kris chortled. "Serves him right. His job is fumigating vermin. Takes a rat to know one!"

I laughed, enjoying the sight of Benjamin's new position.

The station went to local weather, which forecasted a clear day, and with snow on the ground, a white Christmas.

"The dirtbag lost his rental license!" Kris came back on the phone. "Awesome. And Benjamin is done vandalizing property and menacing staff."

"Pest control could be his true calling." I giggled. "That is wonderful! Now the residents can have a safe place to live."

"Absolutely. Can I bring anything to your aunt's home tomorrow? You said not to, but I want to bring something."

"When Auntie invites people to a party, she wants your company, nothing else."

"I'll bring wine."

"Wine is always acceptable," I agreed. "Aunt Liz said she has invited someone from her pickleball group. It may be another one of her setups." I groaned.

"I thought she was giving you a break after the last guy," Kris said. "She'd worn you down."

"Aunt Liz hasn't said anything. I'm reading between the lines," I admitted.

"How's the hot maintenance guy?" She asked with a giggle.

"Still hot." I admitted. "I did ask him to come to Aunties. "The image of Joel, with his flannel work shirt, dimples, and wavy brown hair, flashed along with a sensation of warmth.

"So, we'll see him tomorrow?" she asked.

"No. Long story short. We had a fight and I uninvited him."

"Oh. Sorry."

"Then we made up yesterday."

"Okay." She sounded hopeful.

"But he had already made other plans. I blew it. I have never been very good at relationships."

"Do not worry. It's understandable that he made other plans," she said. "We'll meet him another time."

"Who are the 'we' you keep referring to?"

"Me?" she asked coyly.

"Yes, you. You have referred to yourself as a 'we,' as 'we'll' meet him tomorrow, or another time, twice now."

"Well, we'll have to wait until tomorrow." She gave a full-throated laugh. "Bye." And hung up.

"No fair, Kris," I said to dead air and harrumphed. "Fido, we have work to do."

I had Aunt Liz's gift bag to stuff. Joel's present, a long scarf that would match his eyes and a catnip toy for Tom Kat, needed wrapping. Not to mention the stocking I had to fill for Fido. That would take the bulk of my day while I fretted about whether I had destroyed any promise of a future with Joel.

Chapter 34

Merry

THE DAY OF AUNT Liz's party was bright but cool. A light dusting of snow fell overnight and glistened on the trees, brightening the day. The roadways were clear and dry by afternoon. I loaded my car with the carrot cake bars, rolls, Aunt Liz's present, and Fido, and headed over to her townhouse. There was a little ache in my heart that Joel was not coming. I banished the thought with good food and meeting Aunt Liz and her pickleball friend. And just who was Kris bringing? Our friendship had suffered through the turmoil of job losses, and we no longer had every day to catch up on our lives. I missed her.

"It's wonderful to see you!" Aunt Liz flung open the door, welcoming me. She took the dessert from my arms. I unleashed Fido, who awaited his pet and a treat. After they greeted each other, she stood and waved over a handsome, sturdy gentleman. He had a mass of graying silver hair, and bushy eyebrows over deep-set brown eyes, a mustache, and goatee. He wore a gray argyle sweater over a maroon-colored shirt.

"This is Lucas, my friend from pickleball," she said.

"Please, call me Luke." He gripped my hand firmly. His tanned, squared face stretched into a smile, reaching dark brown eyes.

I blinked. "So nice to meet you," I said.

"You as well. Lizzie has told me so much about you," he said in a deep baritone.

"Really? Hope it is all good." I chuckled. "I have a couple of items left in the car. Be right back."

"It's all terrific! Can I help you?" Luke asked with an amiable smile.

"No, I'm good." On my trip to the car, my thoughts whirled. Who was Luke, and why was he so comfortable calling Aunt Liz, *Lizzie?*

I grabbed the croissants and Aunt Liz's present. Back inside, I offered my gift bag to her. "This is for you. It's our usual." I giggled. Our traditional gifts to each other were fuzzy holiday slippers.

"Oh, you shouldn't have!" she said, laughing, and took the bag and placed it under an enormous Christmas tree while I brought the rolls to the kitchen. Luke stood aside, watching our activities. Aunt Liz and I huddled over the serving dishes, and she asked, "Luke, maybe you could start the fireplace while we set the table." He took the hint and left. I raised my brows with a grin. "So, Luke is a hunk."

"Is he?" She feigned surprise, with a coy smile. "I hadn't noticed."

"Uh, huh." The doorbell rang, and she went to answer.

"Happy holidays!" It was Kris' buoyant voice, and I joined Aunt Liz at the entry. Kris bustled in along with a portly, short, balding man, and a cheerful smile. "Thank you for having us!" Her emerald eyes twinkled, and her red hair shined.

"Here." Kris offered a bottle of champagne with a red bow. "For whenever."

"Wonderful. Thank you. So happy you could join us!" Aunt Liz said. Her voice was breathless, warm. They slipped off coats, and I hung them in the entry closet.

Kris turned to the man with her, dressed in a sports coat. "This is Felix. Felix Bigg." My eyes widened, and I looked mute at her. She fluttered her lashes.

He chimed in, "You must be Merry."

"I am." Remembering my manners, I added, "So nice to meet you. Kris and I worked for the company TREM bought out. You worked with Benjamin." I flushed red, thinking maybe this was not the time or place.

"Yes. I did work with Benjamin. Sad case, that fellow."

"Gorgeous tree!" Kris exclaimed and nudged Felix, turning to Aunt Liz. "You have a beautiful home." Felix murmured 'yes,' in agreement.

"Thank you," Aunt Liz said. "I will put this champagne on ice while you folks mingle."

"I'll help you," I said. Aunt Liz retrieved an ice bucket from a cupboard while I took a bag of ice from the freezer, and I related in a low tone, "So, this is Mr. Bigg, the broker who does all the big real estate deals." She held the bucket while I poured the ice. "*The* Mr. Bigg."

"The more, the merrier." The doorbell rang again. "Would you mind getting that, Merry, while I finish up?" She beamed.

"Sure." Fido had been remarkably well-behaved with all the unfamiliar faces, but he began barking in earnest. I picked him up on the way to the door. Opening the door, I stopped, stunned. "You said you had another invitation!"

"I did. Your aunt called me." Joel grinned. "Can I come in?" The sun shined behind him and highlighted his form. Overtaken by emotion, I stepped aside. With a bottle of wine in one hand, he brushed in, threw his free arm around me and Fido, and kissed my cheek. He whispered, "I'm so happy to see you."

"Me too." I inhaled and felt my toes curl in my shoes. "Happy you're here." We stood in a group hug with Fido, until there was a yip, and Aunt Liz cleared her throat. We jumped apart, and I let Fido down.

"So nice you could come, Joel," Aunt Liz said.

"Thank you for inviting me," he said, slipping off his coat, revealing a deep red sweater.

"It's a pleasure." Smiling, she reached for his coat and hung it in the coat closet. "Merry, give our guests a tour of the house and lower level. Dinner will be ready soon."

"I've had the tour," Luke said. "I'll give you a hand in the kitchen." Placing a hand on Aunt Liz's shoulder, he guided her out of the room.

"I would love your help." She nodded.

"Ooh, I would love a tour," Kris said, eyeing me with a grin.

"Me, too," Felix chimed.

"Lead the way." Joel opened his arms wide.

"Outside of the kitchen and dining room, you are looking at the first level. The view of the river is the best," I said, and gestured to the window.

"It's beautiful," Kris said. Felix nodded his agreement.

"I can show you the lower level. There is a walkout to the river with another view." I headed to the stairs. Joel came behind me, and Felix took Kris's arm, and we trooped downstairs to the family room.

"Gorgeous!" Kris exclaimed. A leather sofa sectional occupied the space in front of a stone fireplace. Outside of the walkout, a patio area with lights adorning evergreens framed the view of the river. A bar, kitchenette, and powder room were at one side of the family room. Through French doors was a guest bedroom.

"Someone could live down here," Joel said.

"Uh huh, in style!" Kris exclaimed. Felix chuckled and looked up at the redhead.

"Someone did," I said with a grimace. "And someone might again." Fido had followed us down and whined at my legs. I picked him up while Joel studied the scenic river.

"Dinner is served!" Luke called from upstairs. "I have been commanded to summon everyone!" I could hear Aunt Liz's giggle in the background. We trooped upstairs, where she said, "Sit anywhere you like; I'll get the rolls." I followed her to the kitchen, and asked in a low tone, "What, no one from the knitting club?"

"They were such downers at Thanksgiving." She shook her head. "Tsk." She sniffed.

"It is the season of forgiveness, Aunt Liz." I looked at her, questioning.

"I forgive them, but that doesn't mean I have to invite them to my home," she said. "Things change. I play pickleball now." She winked and gave a cheerful laugh.

"Luke seems very nice." I raised my brows.

"He is." She smiled innocently.

"Okay. So, how did you get Joel's number?" I frowned while I got out the dog dish.

"I have my ways," she mused, grabbing the basket of rolls. She paused, and added, "It wasn't hard. I called the rental number on the building sign."

"Of course you did. We were on the outs, Aunt Liz. It could have been a disaster, seeing him here."

"Like you said, it is the season of forgiveness. I am glad you made up, dearie," she whispered and went to the dining room with the food.

"Me too." I grinned and put Fido's food down.

With everyone seated at the table, Aunt Liz at the head and Luke at the far end, she raised a glass of champagne.

"Today we are celebrating the holiday, and I raise a glass to new friends. Welcome to my home." She lifted her champagne flute. "And thank you to Kris and Felix for this fabulous bubbly." She sipped.

"Here, here!" we all chimed in and drank, then started to feast.

Felix was the first to break the silence and focused on Joel. "Kris says that you manage apartment buildings. I know where there is an opening for a good apartment manager. I've parted ways with TREM and want a fresh start with someone who respects residents over financial gain."

"Felix is making major changes with his businesses," Kris gushed.

"TREM was the rotten apple in the bushel, you might say." He raised his eyebrows. "With Kris' influence, I am a new man. No more TREM." He raised his glass and smiled.

"That's wonderful!" I spoke. "Reindeer Falls needs reputable apartment owners."

"Okay, this is a holiday dinner. No more business talk," Kris interrupted. Felix reached for her hand.

"It's okay," Joel said. "I have news too. Drum roll, please." He grinned, looked over at me, and paused. "You are looking at the new owner of the buildings on Holly Street and Ivy Lane." I choked and left my fork in the mashed potatoes, taking a napkin to my mouth.

"What?" I asked, nonplussed. "How?"

"The Goldmans and I had an arrangement," he said casually, beaming.

"What kind of arrangement?" I asked with a frown.

"I managed the buildings until I obtained financing to buy," he said. He looked at me. "I had to be sure all my ducks were lined up before I said anything."

"How can you qualify?" I blurted the first thing that came to mind, then I flushed, realizing it wasn't any of my business.

"In my life as a financial manager, I learned that staring at a computer all day wasn't for me," he said.

"Boy, I can relate to that." I chuckled, lifting my glass.

"I saved my money from that high-pressure job. When I started caretaking, my living expenses became less, along with a salary and an apartment. Winning the Reindeer Falls Holiday challenge money clinched the deal with your help. Thank you. Here is to you and your talents." He raised his glass.

"I am flattered and delighted we won!" Nodding, I sipped my drink and smiled.

"Nice," Kris said. "Plus, you have a resident cat," she quipped.

"Tom Kat is just one benefit." He laughed.

"That's right! How is Tom Kat?" I asked.

"He has become a bit of a bum, lounging about the apartment. With the weather, he hasn't been out on the fire escapes, window peeping." He laughed.

"Tom Kat is a character." I giggled, remembering his antics. "He gave Fido a treat once."

"He's a great cat," Joel agreed.

"Who wants dessert?" Aunt Liz asked. "Carrot cake bars, homemade. Merry made them."

"I can recommend the frosting," Joel said with a grin.

"Ooh. Baked goods. Really, you made them?" Kris teased. Her eyes lit up as she spoke. I feigned humility and fluttered my eyelashes.

"I'd love one," Felix said.

"Uh huh, me too!" Luke said.

"So, bars all around," I said. "I'll get them."

"Coffee anyone?" Aunt Liz asked. She rose, and we gathered dinner plates.

"Perfect," Luke said, and sent her a flirty smile, and she blushed.

"Luke really likes you," I whispered, while I cut bars and placed them on dessert plates. Aunt Liz loaded dinner plates in the dishwasher, "Shush. We are working on *your* love life, and Joel is smitten with you." She straightened and placed her hands on her hips. "Perfect, in a word." She gushed.

"We'll see." I was cautious. Joel had not told me about his arrangement with the Goldmans, and a thought nagged at what else hadn't he told me. My heart had been broken before, and I had to keep a rein on my emotions. Although it was becoming more and more difficult with the time we spent together, rehabbing the apartment, decorating the entries, and the drama of the vandalism and fire. I was still determined to move.

"I don't think I've seen you glow this much, even when things were good with Derrick," Aunt Liz said.

"Hmm," I smiled at her. I loaded a tray with the plated desserts and returned to the dining room with Aunt Liz carrying a coffeepot behind me. She filled cups while I served the bars.

Luke was the first to try the dessert, and he groaned. "This is the best bar ever!" he proclaimed.

"Yes, they are the yummiest!" Joel declared.

"Agreed." Kris chortled, and Felix nodded.

Everyone lingered over coffee and dessert, and we adjourned to the family room where Aunt Liz fed the fireplace with wood with help from Luke.

With bantering over the next few hours, it was closing in on six o'clock and dark outside when Felix and Kris glanced at each other, stood, and said, "This has been wonderful," Felix said.

"Thank you so much for inviting us," Kris added.

"I'm so glad you came," she said.

"It was great meeting you, Felix," I said. "We'll chat soon," I added, addressing Kris. We hugged, and they left.

"Thank you so much for having everyone," I said. "I'll help you finish with clean-up, and Fido and I will be out of your hair."

"Nonsense, everything is done," Aunt Liz said. "I'll get your gifts."

Out of the corner of my eye, I saw Joel rise. He joined me. "Yes. I believe Tom Kat is waiting for his staff," he joked. "Thank you, Liz. This has been wonderful. Dinner was fabulous."

"You're welcome," she said. She took out two gift bags from under the tree while I collected coats.

"Thank you! Fido will love this." I peeked in his bag, saw a squeaky toy, and gave her a hug. "It was good meeting you," I waved to Luke, who had settled in the armchair next to the fireplace and tended the fire. He grinned and boomed, "My pleasure!"

We trooped outside. The river walk was lit up with white lights and the arches over the bridge were silhouetted against the night sky. The air was crisp. Joel followed me to my car and helped load. When he folded me in his powerful arms and I felt his breath against my cheek, my stomach dipped. He leaned in for a kiss and added, "I'll follow you home."

At home, Joel helped carry the packages while I retrieved Fido. We trekked up to my floor, and I stopped in my tracks a few feet from my door.

"Derrick! What are you doing here?" I exclaimed. He sat on the floor outside my door, his head in his hands, and lumbered to his feet. His eyes were red and swollen, his gaze unsteady.

"What do you mean, Merry? Waiting on you." He slurred his words, and I asked, exasperated, "Have you been drinking?"

"Just a little." He showed his hands with two fingers, measuring an imaginary drink.

"You can't come in," I warned.

"Aw, Merry," he whined.

"Hey, buddy, let's get you home." Joel stepped forward. I unlocked the door, and he left the packages on the table. He said in a low tone, "I'll handle this." Gripping Derrick's arm and supporting his weight, he walked him down the stairs.

After they left, a little bell went off in my head, and curious, I headed to the laundry room to check out the breaker box, and I exhaled, relieved. It was untouched. I returned to my place, where Joel waited outside my door.

"What happened?" I asked, anxious.

"Got him a cab, sent him home," he said.

"Good. That was fast. Thank you." I shook my head. "This was never like Derrick," I said. "He was never a drinker, or druggie, or anything like that."

"Holidays can be tough." He shrugged. "Hope he can get his act together, because you're my girl now."

"What?" I blushed a deep red.

"I love you, Merry Ernst." He held me in his arms and looked deep into my eyes. I blinked, my heart melted, and he drew me close, kissing me softly.

"I love you, too, Joel Connor." I murmured and held him tight.

Joel

After watching Merry at dinner, I could not contain myself. I had to say it, man up. I loved this woman and want to spend the rest of my life with her. It was fast, but I did not want to lose her. What was I waiting for? She was perfect. She loved the apartments. With her heart and drive, we could make a great life together.

It is time she met the family.

Chapter 35

Merry

I WAS IN LOVE, deliriously and completely. I smiled constantly and was annoyingly cheerful to everyone. The sun was bright, Fido was behaving himself on our walks, and Joel and I saw, or talked to, each other constantly.

"I want you to meet my aunt and uncle, Merry," Joel said. "The people who raised me."

"I'd love to," I said. "When?"

"And there is something I've been meaning to tell you." He sent an apologetic smile.

"Okay?" My stomach churned.

"You've already met them."

"What?" I frowned and shook my head.

"Mr. and Mrs. Goldman are my aunt and uncle."

"The landlords?" My forehead creased, thinking of the short couple that managed the building, then I laughed. "That must be your mother's side of the family. You're nearly six feet."

"Five feet ten and a half, barefoot." He grinned. "You got it. Connor is the Irish Catholic part, my dad. I was raised Catholic until I went to live with the relatives, then it was more the Jewish faith."

"Wow. That must have been quite a change."

"It was. I think that was part of why I acted out. Not only had I lost my parents, but the rituals changed from what I had as a child. I was a scared teenager."

"I'm so sorry you went through that." Then, it hit me, "You mean you could have stopped my eviction all this time?" I asked, feeling betrayed.

"Honest. I tried." He raised his hands. "They only budged after Fido alerted the residents. They still owned the buildings. It was their rules," he said. "Now, not so much. I close on the buildings the first of the year. Fido and you are now preferred residents."

"Hmm." I looked at him, my ire up. "Did they ever find out who messed with the breakers?" I asked, still smarting from the inspector's interrogation.

"I haven't heard. Property crimes are low on the list for police to investigate. No one was hurt, except for Mr. Baker, and that was a heart attack. Police focus on crimes against people."

"Makes sense." I nodded. "Still, it would be nice if the residents did not think I had anything to do with the breaker. I *am* moving." I was firm and had boxes stacked in the living room, ready to move in with Aunt Liz. My bank account was dwindling, and it was time to get serious about my job search.

***

There was a posting on my door one afternoon when I got in from grocery shopping.

"Come, welcome Mr. Baker home!" It went on:

"Mr. Baker cordially invites all residents to his apartment for an afternoon of coffee and treats to celebrate his homecoming and the New Year. Please come celebrate with us." And it was signed Anita, (Mr. Baker's daughter).

A handwritten note under the text said, "We would love for you to bring Fido."

"How nice!" I exclaimed. "We're invited to a party, Fido, this Saturday, New Year's Eve Day." He yipped.

It was Wednesday afternoon when the phone rang. I winced—Derrick, again.

"Merry, thank you for answering." He sounded contrite.

"Okay?" I waited.

"I want to apologize for my behavior at Christmas and earlier. I am sorry."

"Okay, Derrick. Thank you for calling."

"Upon the advice of my sisters, I've started AA."

"That's great, Derrick."

"I want to be truthful about everything."

"Okay?" I waited, puzzled.

"I tampered with the breaker box."

"Oh, Derrick!"

"I know, I know." He sounded miserable. "It was a stupid thing to do, irrational. I don't know how I can make up for it. I thought nothing would happen. When I heard about the apartment fire, I felt awful."

"Derrick, tell the fire inspector what you just told me."

There was a long silence.

"Okay, Merry. I will do that." He sounded resigned.

"I'll give you his name and number." Finding the card, I rattled off the number. "Good luck to you."

"Please forgive me, Merry, for everything," he said.

"I forgive you. Thank you for telling me the truth." After I hung up, relief flooded me. The mystery of who had tampered with the breaker box was solved. I did not know if Derrick would follow through with the inspector, and I didn't know what they would do, but I was happy that he took responsibility for messing with the breakers. I wished him the best. My invisible barrier slipped away, and smiling, I hung up.

***

Fido and I walked up to Mr. Baker's apartment. The door was ajar, and I heard voices from inside. I pushed open the door, and a cheer went out.

"There they are!" Mr. Baker greeted us where he stood beside the table filled with several kinds of cookies and brownies. A woman was beside him. Their resemblance was uncanny, with salt and pepper hair, round cherubic faces, and big smiles.

"I'm Anita, his daughter," she said. "Are you Merry?"

"Yes."

"And this is Fido?"

"It is." I smiled.

"He's a hero," she said. "I am so glad there was a dog in the building, and that he smelled the smoke and alerted everyone. It meant so much for Dad's outcome."

"And to the rest of us!" another woman called out. "We could have been toast!"

"Thank you!" The comments thrilled me, and I stroked Fido, who had become shy and held back at my ankles.

Joel strolled in with Tom Kat on his shoulders. The cat nuzzled Joel's neck and eyed Fido. The cat and dog stared at each other.

"I think they're getting used to each other, living in harmony," Joel said, and grinned. He stroked the cat.

"Could be." I smiled at the two. My heart sang at Joel's presence. I brought Fido up to my shoulders and offered the dog and cat a chance to sniff. Fido was curious and went first. Tom Kat leaned away, then met him nose to nose.

"See?" Joel grinned. We smiled giddily at each other until a short woman pushed her way into the apartment behind Joel. He turned and introduced a couple who entered. "Merry, I think you know my aunt and uncle."

"Mr. and Mrs. Goldman! So nice to see you again," I exclaimed.

"Please, call me Nate," the short man said and held out his hand.

"And I'm Stella," the taller of the two said in a deep voice. "It's a pleasure to know Joel's girl." I flushed at her greeting.

"We didn't want it out that Joel is our nephew because he had to learn the ropes on his own," Nate said. "Better for him to make his own mark."

"And he has done that. He has done a fine job," Stella said. "With some help. This apartment looks marvelous." She grinned at me and Fido.

"Thanks, guys," Joel said. "Let's eat."

"Looks good." Nate viewed the desserts and patted his stomach. "I could eat."

"Me, too," Stella agreed. "I'm happy you found each other." She took my hand, and squeezed it, and they moved to the table laden with food.

"Looks like you passed muster," Joel whispered.

"How's that?" I asked.

"They couldn't stand to be in the same room with Patricia," he said in a low tone, sheepish.

"Really? Why?" I frowned.

"Not sure. I think there was an intuition that we were not a good match," he said. "They were right."

We spent the next couple of hours mingling with residents as they came and went. It thrilled many to meet Fido, and they stroked him cautiously. After we had had our fill of holiday cookies, Joel turned to me and winked, grabbing my elbow. "Let's go back to your place. The party is almost over," he whispered, squeezing my hand.

He spoke so quickly that I didn't have time to ponder. "Okay."

He turned to the partygoers and said, "Thank you, everyone, for a wonderful get together, and I wish everyone a healthy and happy New Year!" He plucked Tom Kat from where the cat perched on the back of Mr. Baker's armchair, and I gathered Fido. We continued to say our goodbyes as we ducked out of the party.

Laughing, we made our way back to my place and sat in the living room. Fido was on the sofa beside us and Tom Kat on the sofa back.

"Do you want something to drink?" I asked, settling into the couch cushions.

"Maybe," he said. "It all depends—" He rose and lifted a small jewelry case from his pants pocket. He pushed the coffee table away and went to one knee. My eyes widened, and I gasped, seeing the case. He opened the box to a solitaire diamond engagement ring.

"Will you be my wife, my forever home designer?" he asked.

Speechless, I stared.

"Will you marry me?"

"Yes!" He brought the ring out and placed it on my ring finger.

He gazed at me and held my hands in his, and I knew I had the same deer in the lights look I had the night of the fire.

"Yes," I said. "I will be your forever designer. I will marry you."

We kissed, long and deep.

In the background, Tom Kat had leaped to the couch, where he and Fido snuggled together. The cat opened one eye, yawned, burrowed next to Fido, and fell back to sleep.

Chapter 36

Merry

IT WAS A WHIRLWIND romance, and we spent the next six months getting to know each other. I stayed at my apartment on Holly Street, while Joel and I navigated our new love for each other. Joel and Fido came to accept each other, and Fido and Tom Kat developed a sibling canine/feline relationship. If Fido could talk, he would likely have some words about Tom Kat's ability to leap to different heights. Something Fido couldn't ever master. Tom Kat would never have the feisty, loud bark that Fido had.

The next few months flew by. I sat for my real estate sales license exam and was excited to pass with no problem. Together, Joel and I managed Holly Street and Ivy Lane apartment homes with a special emphasis on redesigning spaces to suit new tenants.

In June, Joel and I pledged our vows in the yard of Aunt Liz's villa, facing the river under a white trellis, adorned with flowers. It was a lovely spring day, and her friend, Luke, helped her host the wedding. Kris and Felix attended, along with the knitter club members, who eyed Luke like Tom Kat would a bird.

As she helped me dress for the occasion and fussed around my dress, Aunt Liz remarked, "Well, now I can rest easy with the promise I made to your mother. We came in under the wire, with time to spare, with you turning twenty-seven now. I made it happen," she said smugly.

"Aunt Liz," I protested, "How do you figure? I met Joel at my building. You did not make a match."

"Who found the pet-friendly building, dearie?" She arched a brow.

"You did," I said. "But," I sputtered, "you didn't introduce us."

"Close enough!" she said. And that was the end of that.

The End

Acknowledgements

Many people deserve my gratitude for their support, friendship, and work associated with The Perfect Match. My sincere thank you to the following: Betty Borns, for her steady encouragement and support, Cousin Wayne, who challenged me to write a romance, Tom Kat, the neighborhood stray, and Chipper, (my Morkie) who sparked the idea. The SINC guppies who said, 'do it.' Beta reader Judith Anne Horner, and other readers who made this a better book. Cathy Buchholz, William Anderson, and the Twin City Sisters in Crime for their support of local writers. Librarians and booksellers who recommend my work.

Most of all, I am grateful for my husband, Joe, who cheerfully travels with me on this journey.

About the author

The Perfect Match is the first romance novel penned by M. E. Bakos. She hopes you will enjoy celebrating the holiday season with Joel, Merry, Tom Kat, and Fido in quaint Reindeer Falls.

Mary lives in Minnesota with her husband, Joe, and a spoiled pooch named Chipper.

You can reach her at mebakos@yahoo.comOn Facebook: https://www.facebook.com/mebakos/

https://www.facebook.com/mary.sebesta.90/ Website: https://mebakos.wixsite.com/author

She loves hearing from readers!

Also by

Get cozy with A Home Renovator Mystery!
The series is set in fictional Crocus Heights, Minnesota, and revolves around a feisty home flipper turned sleuth.
Buy in E-book or print at your favorite bookseller.
Fatal Flip, Deadly Flip, Lethal Flip, Killer Flip, and Mortal Flip.

www.ingramcontent.com/pod-product-compliance
Lightning Source LLC
LaVergne TN
LVHW091718070526
838199LV00050B/2452